NITT-WITT RIDGE

A Big Sur Freak Fable

1/1/08

For Ted & Denise
(& Mama when she's older...)
on New Year's Eve, 2008.

Thanks for the extra
set of earmuffs. They
made all the difference
when JiJi was braving
the fireworks. Here's
to good friends and
good times ahead.

CRASH GORDON

Hope you like the book

Danen

NITT-WITT RIDGE is a work of fiction. When the names of "real" places, corporations, institutions, and public figures are projected onto *Nitt-Witt Ridge's* fictional landscape, they are used fictitiously. All other names, characters, locales, and events are products of the author's imagination or, at best, scribbled missives from the collective unconscious. Any apparent similarity to actual persons, living or dead or otherwise occupied is entirely coincidental.

The same applies to Derek Swannson's Introduction, as well....

Author's Note: There's one exception to the disclaimer above. The portrait of Captain Nitt-Witt is based on my many encounters with Art Beal, the original Captain Nitt-Witt (pictured on the book's cover). Art approved of everything I wrote about him. "You see things in re-*AL*-ity," he once told me—a high compliment coming from a cantankerous old fart who lived alone in a nine-story castle of beer cans and abalone shells that was rigged with dynamite to explode whenever he felt like testing his theories on the transmigration of souls.

P.S. That bit of dialogue toward the bottom of Page 90 about fish eyelids atrophying due to the evolutionary benefits of googly-eyed terror comes from Art's good friend, Peter Fels.

In memory of

Art Beal

(1896-1992)

the original

Captain Nitt-Witt

FIRST EDITION

ISBN-10: 0-9799105-2-8

ISBN-13: 978-0-9799105-2-4

Contents

INTRODUCTION

Crash Gordon, the author of *Nitt-Witt Ridge*, is my big brother—but I didn't know him very well when I was growing up. We were thirteen years apart and Crash just disappeared one day around the time I turned four. Everyone thought he was dead. Three of his friends had been killed when their car went over a cliff in Big Sur. Crash had been with them, but his body was never found. The police told us that if the fall hadn't killed him, then he most likely drowned. Either way, his body must have been swept out to sea on the tide.

They were wrong, as it turned out. Six years later Crash showed up again in Kingsburg, California—our hometown. His blonde hair had grown out into a wild, shaggy mane and he was wearing a grey, musty-smelling wizard's cloak—or monk's habit— that he'd picked up for sixty *kroner* in a Norwegian thrift shop. He had a long, weird story to tell about waking up in a Monterey hospital with amnesia, then spending the next five years at the Esalen Institute attending seminars and developing his trippy psychic abilities. There was also something about a Tantric sex tour in Europe.

Most people, listening to him, must have thought he'd gone a little nuts. I know our mother did. She wouldn't let him stay in our house. But Crash was my brother, and I wanted to believe him, so I asked him to tell me more.

Over the years, Crash ended up telling me *a whole lot* more. And what he told me was so funny and frightening and bizarre that I eventually decided to write a book about it. Six years and more than six hundred pages later, that book was published by Three Graces Press as *Crash Gordon and the Mysteries of Kingsburg*.

It was my first book and it's been such a success that I'm already working on a sequel: *Crash Gordon and the Revelations from Big Sur*. Crash doesn't seem to mind. I'm not quite sure why he puts up with me cannibalizing his life for the sake of "Quality Lit"—as Terry Southern called it—but I think it's probably because he wanted to be a novelist himself when he was younger.

In fact, Crash wrote a 332-page apprentice novel called *Blind and Hairless* when he was only sixteen. I remember him giving me a piggyback ride down to the local drugstore for a hot fudge sundae on the day that he finished it, not long before he disappeared. Later, we went over to our grandmother's house to tell her all about it.

The main character in *Blind and Hairless* is a bald-headed juvenile delinquent named Eddie who has telekinetic powers because he wasn't breast-fed as a child. There are dramatic conflicts inherent in that situation, of course. As I had Crash explain it to our grandmother in *my* first book:

"The telekinetic powers only work when Eddie is grabbing his, um, testicles… which kind of causes problems. So he starts seeing a psychiatrist, this guy named Doctor Ewen Cameron, who doesn't really believe him. He thinks Eddie just has an Oedipus complex. But by the end of the book, the telekinetic powers have started attacking Eddie. They actually make him blind and hairless. Then they attack Doctor Cameron who, through the process of transference, finds out that he has telekinetic powers, too, which kind of drives him nuts—because it blows his faith in an intelligible universe. So Doctor Cameron ends up stumbling around like a bum, searching for a non-rational way of understanding the world and his place in it.

"Meanwhile, Eddie and his best friend, George—who's, like, this weird, redheaded, six-foot-seven retarded milk truck driver—they, um, drive out to the river in George's old milk truck and Eddie asks George to shoot his testicles off with a .357 Magnum. When the telekinetic powers hear that they stir up a windstorm that turns into a tornado and then there's a rain of fecal greaseballs and the milk truck

flies up into the sky, spilling milk bottles everywhere. But George is brave and he manages to pull the trigger and blow Eddie's balls off in an act of true friendship. Eddie sits down bleeding under a pine tree, the tornado stops, and the fecal greaseballs turn into bread and start baking in the sun. And everyone gets to live happily ever after.... I mean, that's it in a nutshell, but there's a lot more to it and it's way more complicated, of course."

It was one hell of a book to have written when he was only sixteen (and more autobiographical and predictive of his future than you might at first think), but Crash obviously wasn't dealing with universal themes. Not everyone could relate to it. The manuscript was left behind in a desk drawer in his old room back in Kingsburg, never to be published. I read it when *I* was sixteen, and I thought it was great—kind of a cross between John Steinbeck's *Of Mice and Men* and Stephen King's *Carrie*—but by then I was hopelessly biased. Crash was my mysterious older brother, recently returned from the dead, and I couldn't help but look up to him.

Crash wrote a second book, *The Sensuous Hermit,* while he was recovering from amnesia at the Esalen Institute in Big Sur. Richard Price, one of Esalen's founders, had offered him free room and board there, for as long as he wanted to stay, in exchange for letting them use him as a psychic guinea pig. Crash was especially talented at remote viewing—basically, sitting alone in a dark room and describing what's happening at a remote location, after being given no more information about that location than its longitude and latitude. I know it sounds crazy, but the military and the CIA have been using remote viewers to find crashed planes, spy on the Russians, and track down Middle Eastern terrorists ever since the early 1970s. Crash was supposedly trained to do remote viewing—and other things, like remote influencing—in a CIA-sponsored mind control program while he was growing up.

No wonder our mom wouldn't let him stay in the house, right?

But here's the thing: there was corroborating evidence for Crash's abilities. I've heard him predict things that later came true more times than I can even count. And once, during the summer before I started college, I was hanging out in Crash's cabin drawing a picture and when I went out to tell him I'd chugged the last three beers in his refrigerator, I found him sitting at the picnic table on his deck drawing *the exact same picture*. I was so blown away that I went back inside and drew a dozen more pictures, as an experiment. Without any way of seeing me, or even knowing what I was doing, Crash drew perfect reproductions of all twelve—even the one of the silicone-enhanced alien girl and her basset hound sidekick, who was up on his hind legs in a filthy raincoat with a fedora tilted at a rakish angle over one eye, French-inhaling a cigarette.

And then there's the anecdotal evidence, which wouldn't be admissible in court, but still... it's impressive. For instance, over the years I've heard *this* story from at least three different witnesses who all claim they were there when it happened:

Kurt Vonnegut was on a book tour in California when he decided to stop by the Esalen Institute to see what their "human potential movement" was all about. This was sometime around 1984 or '85, I was told. There was a seminar going on in the Big House that day about the *siddhis*—the occult bodily powers that arise along the path to enlightenment. Vonnegut smelled bullshit and at one point he stood up and said:

"Anyone here who believes in telekinetics, raise my hand."

Crash was standing across the room, and he was having one of his fluky moments when his remote influencing abilities were running particularly strong, so he raised Vonnegut's hand for him.

I guess old Kurt just about shit a brick.

Anyway, to get back to *The Sensuous Hermit*... Crash was obviously using the manuscript to organize his returning memories. It was structured around the somewhat loopy notion that there are four distinct stages to any successful hermit's life: the Budding Hermit, the Reluctant Hermit, the Traditional Hermit, and the Sensuous Hermit. It's a strange read—a bit too gnomic for my taste, especially in the last section—but you can definitely see how Crash was trying to fit his life experiences into a template, so he could make better sense of them.

Crash's childhood was pretty bleak—I know that much from personal experience. Our mom was a pill-popping nudist with a violent temper. Once, she smacked me across the skull with a pooper-scooper (seventeen stitches and a really bad infection…). I'm sure she did about the same or even worse to Crash. Our emotionally aloof dad flew a Cessna into his own living room on the day after Crash's thirteenth birthday. No one knew if it was an accident or suicide (or maybe a misguided attempt to murder his wife…). I'd been conceived about eight months earlier, so I never had a chance to meet the guy, but Crash was the first person on the scene when the plane hit our house. He found our dad's dismembered corpse, which must've really screwed with his head. And then, to top it all off, there was that cliff in Big Sur a few years later where he lost three of his closest friends.

All that stuff got written about, allegorically, in *The Sensuous Hermit* as it was dredged up from the murk and muck of Crash's receding amnesia. No wonder he wanted to become a hermit!

If you ask me, I don't think Crash ever intended to publish *The Sensuous Hermit*. It was probably just something he had to get out of his system. The whole thing comes across as a sarcastic self-help guide for misanthropes, interspersed with true-to-life stories about those awkward moments and small (and large) humiliations that the world doles out on a regular basis. The plot is sort of a smutty *Pilgrim's Progress* that follows an alienated young man through childhood, sexual maturity, and existential despair—and then on to something like orgasmic enlightenment. But that last part, for me at least, remains vague. It has something to do with transcending the duality of spirituality and sensuality by masturbating into a tuna sandwich, and frankly, I just don't get it.

After Crash had finished writing the manuscript, he packed it away in a little antique Chinese leather trunk, packed the trunk in an old beat-to-crap Jeep Wagoneer, and then he left the Esalen Institute to find a new way of life. He didn't know where he was going. He just had the idea that he was becoming too insulated from the rest of the world at Esalen—he obviously had issues, writing a book called *The Sensuous Hermit*—so he struck out for parts unknown. He only got as far as Cambria, about sixty miles down the coast, but it was a start.

What stopped him in Cambria was a radio program. He was just driving along, listening to the local station, when a DJ calling himself A.C. Nightshade came on the air to say, "You're listening to KOTR, wet 'n' furry radio for the Central Coast." Crash instantly recognized the voice as belonging to his childhood friend from Kingsburg, Jimmy Marrsden.[1]

Five years earlier, Jimmy had been in the car with Crash and his three friends for their rendezvous with the cliff in Big Sur. But Crash recalled, dimly, that Jimmy had been standing in the road off to the side of the car just before it smashed through the guardrail. *How had that happened?* He pulled off the highway into Cambria to find Jimmy—or A.C. Nightshade—and talk to him about it.

It turned out to be a very long conversation. Crash spent the next several years in Cambria. For much of that time, he and Jimmy were roommates in the same tiny home.

It wasn't a bad existence... at least, not at first.

With the hippie-academic stench of Esalen still clinging to his wizard cloak, Crash introduced himself to Cambria's demimonde by delivering an impromptu lecture entitled, "Quantum Physics and Reaganomics: How Much Longer Before the Fabric of Reality is Ripped to Shreds?" The lecture took place in Old Camozzi's Saloon on the night of Crash and Jimmy's reunion, after a few too many celebratory gin-and-tonics. By that time, Crash was beyond taking himself seriously. Goaded on by Jimmy, he managed to convince a morose marimba player from a Don Ho-inspired hula band to accompany him while he was up onstage.

"Dancing," Crash suavely slurred into the microphone, *"is encouraged."* He expected he would either be ignored or heckled mercilessly. He was, after all, only going through with the act to amuse an old friend—a round of karaoke for the metaphysics nerds.

Half-eloquently, half-incoherently, Crash riffed on the Holographic Model of the Universe, Zen quarks, Laffer curves on the Feynman momentum-energy space map, and the virtues of raw

---

[1] Some readers of this Introduction may have heard of Jimmy—or at least his pseudonym, A.C. Nightshade (the A.C. stands for either Anti-Christ or Aleister Crowley; Jimmy could never settle on one or the other, so he used both). A.C. Nightshade is the *New York Times* best-selling author of *Vampirism Made Easy* and more than a dozen other books—many of them made into popular movies. But how all that started is a story for another book (the one I'm currently working on...)

oysters and psychedelic mushrooms as counteractive agents against existential despair. By the end of the lecture, to his astonishment, he was drunkenly applauded by the crowd and then embraced by a silver-haired woman with a Boston accent who introduced herself as Nora Biddle-Whitney, owner and editor-in-chief of the *Cambria Insurrectionist*. Right there on the spot, Nora offered Crash a job on her newspaper.

Some find religion. Crash found journalism and he was saved.

Crash has never really explained to me why he went into his hermit tailspin at Esalen. From what he's told me, it sounds like a great place—full of shamanic psychotherapists, braless quantum physicists, and flaky but adorable hippie nymphomaniacs. But I guess Crash couldn't shake the feeling that he was some combination of charity case and circus freak while he was there. He told me that demonstrating his psychic abilities in front of a new crowd always felt embarrassing, like putting on a white cape and jumping out of a birthday cake with his hard-on wagging. He didn't want to do it anymore. So when Nora Biddle-Whitney offered him a new career as a journalist, Crash saw it as a way out. I think he knew, intuitively, that he needed to get past his morbid self-consciousness by devoting his energies to some cause greater than himself. So what if Nora could only pay him $5.50 an hour? He was happy to take it.

Gainfully employed, Crash was able to rent a one-room shingled geodesic dome cabin that nobody wanted because its tenant had to climb a nine-story flight of rickety stairs up the side of a cliff to get to it. But at the top of the cliff, the cabin had a small redwood deck with a magnificent view overlooking Cambria's Moonstone Beach. On a clear day, Crash could see all the way up the coastline to Big Sur—or so he believed. (Realistically, there wasn't much to see but ocean out beyond the lighthouse at Piedras Blancas.)

Crash fell in love with Cambria. He loved the tall, gnarled spires of Monterey pines growing everywhere, making the roads look like wide aisles for altar boys in a shady green cathedral. He loved the beach in front of his cabin—which really *was* full of moonstones—and he loved the tide pools filled with strange sea anemones, purple starfish, and briny clumps of bearded mussels. But what he loved most of all was his new job.

Nora started him out on production paste-up and sent him on a few inconsequential photo assignments. Crash's photos came back looking much better than anyone could have reasonably expected. Soon he was shooting the majority of the *Insurrectionist's* photos and doing most of the darkroom work, too. Nora's previous darkroom technician had decided he had a more lucrative career ahead of him as a tree surgeon. He only hung around long enough to teach Crash the basics. It felt like alchemy to Crash, watching a silver gelatin print come up in the developer tray under the red safelights. He turned out to have a preternatural talent for photography that quickly evolved into a kind of warped greatness.[2]

After Crash was comfortably adept with his new photography chores, Nora started assigning him to do interviews and local color pieces. She suspected Crash could write, based on what she'd heard during his drunken lecture, and the interviews had been her true goal all along. She wasn't disappointed.

Crash started work on a series of interviews that he collectively titled *Cambria Souls*. His inspiration, once again, came from a line by William Blake:

> *The worship of God is Honouring his gifts in other men, each according to his genius, and loving the greatest men best; those who envy or calumniate great men hate God; for there is no other God.*

In Crash's mind, that line provided him with the bent justification he needed to become a "Journalist of the Soul" and go after interviews with some of Cambria's most infamous oddball characters.

The list was long. Cambria seemed to be a magnet for independent thinkers and inspired dreamers. There was Warren

---

[2] Crash's surrealistic photographs wound up being shown in art galleries all over the world and turned into a steady source of income that carried him through the next twenty years. Thank god it worked out that way... otherwise, Crash might've spent the rest of his life on Madame Sophie's crack team of dial-a-psychics, hustling for his cut of 99¢ a minute.

Leopold, the rebel architect, who'd owned and operated a whorehouse up in Alaska with Dashiell Hammett during World War II. And there was Phoebe Palmer, the visionary portrait artist, who rendered the tacky, polyester-clad visitors to Hearst Castle—with their sun-wrinkled skin and flabby bellies—in erotic poses modeled after 11th-century Tantric temple carvings. But perhaps most significantly, there was Art Beal—alias Captain Nitt-Witt—the rabble-rousing folk art genius creator of Nitt-Witt Ridge.[3]

To prepare for his newspaper story about Art Beal, Crash spent a lot of time hanging out on a sprung couch up in Nitt-Witt Ridge's decrepit old crow's nest, just shooting the breeze with Art and watching the sunset. Crash swore that a beautiful calm would sweep over him every time he was up there, making him think, *This is the way life should be lived.*[4]

After the interview with Captain Nitt-Witt was published to great acclaim, Crash started writing the novel that would become *Nitt-Witt Ridge*. He kept up his journalism work in the meantime. By turning local people into celebrities, Crash was becoming a celebrity of sorts himself. He was finally getting some recognition as a writer.

The novel came together slowly over the next three years. Based on his earlier writing efforts, Crash had no reason to think the completed manuscript would change his life in any significant way. Unlike his previous two books, however, this one would be published. Horst Veblin—the shabby genteel publisher of the Cambria-based Owlphart Press—happened to be an avid reader of Crash's newspaper articles. When Horst met Crash at a local bongo drumming party, he assured him that *Nitt-Witt Ridge* sounded like the perfect book to add to Owlphart's roster of neo-surrealist fiction. Crash was ecstatic!

---

[3] I'm not going to spoil Crash's descriptions of Captain Nitt-Witt and Nitt-Witt Ridge by writing about them here. Just know that Captain Nitt-Witt was a real person (Art Beal died in 1992) and Nitt-Witt Ridge remains a real place (it was designated a California Historical landmark back in 1981).

[4] I don't think he knew at the time that the whole place was rigged to explode with dynamite—bundles and bundles of old miner's dynamite, sweating nitroglycerin, which could have gone off at any moment. (The bomb squad had to go in and very carefully dispose of it after Art's death, but that was years later.)

The soon-to-be-bankrupt Owlphart Press picked up *Nitt-Witt Ridge* for a $500 advance (the check bounced) and did an initial print run of 1,000 copies (most of which were destroyed in a warehouse fire suspected to have been started by Horst's cousin, a twice-convicted arsonist).

Poor Crash just never had much luck with his damn novels....

He quit writing books after that. Who could blame him? He might have kept going if it hadn't been for some well-timed discouragement from his undermining friend, Jimmy Marrsden—a.k.a. A.C. Nightshade—whose agent had sold the film rights to Jimmy's unpublished first novel, *Vampirism Made Easy,* for a cool $666,000 on the very day that Crash's books went up in flames. With his ego pumped up beyond all reason, Jimmy told Crash it was probably for the best that *Nitt-Witt Ridge's* entire print run had been torched—because the books wouldn't have sold, anyway. Now, at least, he could collect on the insurance.

Nice, huh?

Some glib malcontent once said that success is always sweeter when it's accompanied by the failure of a friend. I wouldn't know anything about that, but A.C. Nightshade sure does.

The big irony is that a few years earlier, when Jimmy had hit bottom in a full-on alcoholic flameout (a quart of vodka a day, an unfaithful new wife, a chainsaw applied to the conjugal waterbed), he'd moved in with Crash to get his shit together. It was tight quarters with two big, smelly guys living in a one-room cabin, but Crash had gladly put up with Jimmy because he considered him his best friend. They'd worked on their novels together, reading the pages out loud, doing their best to crack each other up. It had been a fun and productive time for both of them—although a little skeevy on the housekeeping front.

With a check for more than half-a-million-dollars on the way to him, Jimmy decided he could finally afford to rent his own place. He moved out over the next weekend, leaving Crash with a lot of unpaid bills. Not much later, he was seen driving a sexy black Ferrari around town with spider web pinstripes and vanity plates that read: NTSHADE.

DCKHEAD would've been more appropriate, if you ask me.

"Success makes assholes of us all," Crash once said to me, in a philosophical mood. He didn't really blame Jimmy for being a jerk, but I did. "Just wait until it happens to you," Crash told me. "You'll do the same. Even Gandhi couldn't please everybody."

Well, maybe.... Look, I know I haven't done enough to end world hunger, provide shelter for the homeless, or find a cure for Lesch-Nyhan syndrome (a disease that causes spastic but strangely personable little boys to bite off the ends of their own fingers). I'm definitely no saint. I probably could have bought five gallons of fresh water and a bucket of government rice for every starving kid in Burkina Faso with all the money I've spent on imported beer. But at least I look out for my friends.

That's why, when Three Graces Press asked me if I knew of any other writers who might benefit from being published by them, I told them about Crash's old incinerated novel, *Nitt-Witt Ridge*. Maybe it could rise, Phoenix-like, from the ashes, I suggested. The guys at Three Graces promised me they'd take a look at it.

Crash was a little skeptical when I told him. He wasn't so sure that publishing a sixteen-year-old novel was such a great idea. I pointed out to him that people still read *Moby-Dick*—and that's a lot older.

"Don Quixote might've been a better example," Crash told me. Then, encouraged by the vision of old Quixote tilting at windmills, he dug up the original manuscript and handed it over.

And now here it is: from my hands to yours. Books are incredibly wonderful things, don't you think?

Reading *Nitt-Witt Ridge* probably won't change your life in any meaningful way, but if you're the right kind of person it can provide you access to an alternate hippie-freak universe that's somewhat kinder and happier than the world we live in now (despite the occasional exploding hamster and the rampaging of a giant, vindictive, chrome robot-rooster). The Pine Bluff of *Nitt-Witt Ridge* is Crash's fictional stand-in for Cambria—a timeless place where computers, cell phones, and right-wing Republicans don't seem to exist. Or as one of Crash's characters imagines it:

In the Pine Bluff of Mickelodia's dreams, no one was ever mean or egotistical. Everyone lived in a web of gentle hippie magic, connected by threads of love and serendipity. The mayor wore blue jeans. The Tao was required reading in high school. The streets were shaded by elms, oak trees, and Monterey pines taller than any buildings. When two grown men couldn't link their hands around a tree's trunk, Pine Bluff threw a party and gave the tree a tire swing. The tire swing count was a source of civic pride. Anyone could tell you the number.

A creek ran through the center of town. You could fish for trout from the back porch of Wilfred Logan's General Store—but you had to use flies. Wilfred disapproved of bait.

Water wheels and solar panels provided most of Pine Bluff's energy. Almost everyone practiced a trade—from blacksmithing to zither stringing—so that very few goods were ever brought in from the big cities. Bartering was a way of life; cash rarely changed hands. Mickelodia imagined she could get everything she needed, which was really very little, by growing a simple garden and bartering her natural skills as a babysitter, a reader of bedtime stories, a gatherer of wildflowers....

Mickelodia makes Pine Bluff sound like a place where I'd like to live—or at least be able to visit. I kind of envy Crash his days with the *Cambria Insurrectionist*. Those days are long gone now and maybe they were never as great as Crash makes them seem. But if the Pine Bluff of Mickelodia's fictional imagining never truly existed, I would argue that it *should* exist. And it does, thanks to Crash's writing. *Nitt-Witt Ridge* may be a shaggy, Brautiganesque bong water bubble of a book, but it's also semi-profound in its own laid back way and laugh-out-loud funny. Or at least I think so.

But what the hell do I know, right?

Maybe A.C. Nightshade had it nailed from the start: the world doesn't need or want a book like *Nitt-Witt Ridge*. Instead, what we need is another book about a vampire girl with perky tits who rips the throat out of a sleeping wino while the wino's scabby, hairless Chihuahua tries to hump her leg. Or a book about demons and the fun they have eating the souls of clueless humans.

But now, at least, you'll have the opportunity to read *Nitt-Witt Ridge* and make that determination for yourself, rather than having A.C. Nightshade decide for you.

I hope you end up liking Crash's book as much as I do.

—Derek Swannson, Summer, 2007

1

HARLEY, HIS INCIPIENT ROOSTERNESS

When Harley Marndog and Calliope Kolankiewicz were married, Harley's grandfather, J. Milford Marndog, gave them the deed to a modest hog farming operation on twenty acres of redwood-forested land outside of Pine Bluff—an old mining town turned tourist trap on the high cliffs of the California coastline just south of Big Sur. Calliope, a vegetarian at the time, insisted the hogs be set free before she moved in with Harley.

Upon their return from a honeymoon in Jamaica, Harley sent his grandfather a comically rueful note complaining about Calliope's wanton disregard for the value of good pork. Included with the note was a conciliatory cigar, which J. Milford promptly smoked. He was a senile old capitalist with a strong yen for bacon, and his daughter-in-law's swine-liberation struck him as wasteful and impertinent. He felt a hot fury boiling off his mottled pink ear tips. Soon, however, he noticed the skunky perfume from Harley's cigar seemed to be putting him in a much better mood. He suddenly didn't care so much about feral pigs and corporate profits. In fact, he decided he would never again be a slave to material desires. As his first act of independence, he flushed his gold Rolex watch down the toilet.

Years later, in his final postcard to Harley and Calliope, J. Milford told them he was herding sheep in Jamaica. He had liquidated his vast industrial empire and traveled there to search for more of Harley's special cigars. He claimed to be the father of seven Jamaican babies—each with surly green eyes, beautiful ebony skin... and a million-dollar trust fund.

"Grandpa Milford's always been a hopeless horndog," said Harley with a grin.

"You'd think at his age he'd know a little something about contraception," said Calliope. "Frankly, I'm surprised he can still get it up."

"He does a whole lot more than just get it up. I've got seven rich Rastafarian baby uncles!"

Harley felt like celebrating. He grabbed Calliope and danced the mambo, right there in his electric blue boxer shorts.

Nine months later, Harley and Calliope were graced with a baby of their own. Philo entered the world to find his parents raising zebras on their land—a decidedly unprofitable venture. Harley had become a tree surgeon to pay the family's bills.

Philo had splendid but unreliable memories of his early childhood. As a baby, he had absolutely no fear of falling. He was quite sure of that. He seemed to recall being packed in a knapsack and carried on his father's back as Harley went about his business. The money saved in babysitter's fees must have been substantial.

On weekends—or so Philo imagined—his mother tied him to the tail of a kite and let the breeze carry him up to the tops of tall redwoods, where his father worked. But Philo longed to go still higher, to commune with the clouds. His mother didn't think it was safe to let out that much string.

Inspired by dirigibles, Philo began retaining gas. He gorged himself on beans, zucchini, and jalapeños—and refused to burp or fart. He also inhaled the helium from numerous birthday party balloons.

Philo grew immense and airy. His thoughts turned grandiose. He would avenge the *Hindenburg*—make the airspace safe for bloated babies!

He started wearing mooring cables on his wrists and ankles. His parents thought it was just a child's harmless affectation until Philo won a trophy in the Macy's Thanksgiving Day Parade.

After that, the cables came off and he wasn't allowed to leave his room until he deflated.

□ □ □ □ □ □ □ □ □

Harley's memories of his own childhood were nowhere near so agreeable. Harley's mother, Charlene, was a big Norwegian woman with a wild temper who had habitually flown into psychotic rages over spilled milk and muddy floors. Harley had spent most of his childhood hiding from her in closets and up in the limbs of tall trees. He had vowed to be a much more mellow parent around Philo.

Charlene, of course, didn't approve of the manner in which Philo was being raised. She saw a lack of discipline turning the boy into "a snot-nosed young hellion." She also felt Philo's moral integrity was being compromised by "the wicked lasciviousness of that Hippie Harlot."

By that latter turn of phrase, she meant Calliope.

Harley had once tried explaining to Charlene that Philo's moral integrity, or lack thereof, was something Philo would have to work out on his own. And just because Calliope had a frank, sensual manner and a voluptuous body that she tended to clothe in peasant skirts and lacy satin bodices, that didn't mean she was a slut.

To which Charlene had responded: "How would you know, Girly Boy?"

Charlene thought Harley's long blonde ponytail somehow compromised his masculinity. She didn't care that Harley climbed trees all day with chainsaws dangling from his hips, that he was highly skilled in a variety of the martial arts, or that his reflexes were so quick that he could punch a flying quail with his fists.

Charlene was, in Harley's long-considered opinion, "A shark-faced bitch with no real life of her own."

□ □ □ □ □ □ □ □ □

Dealing with his tree surgeon business and his hateful shrew of a mother took a lot out of Harley, but he always managed to rejuvenate himself by taking time out to indulge his favorite hobby. To that end, he'd built a laboratory in one of his grandfather's old sheds.

Harley fancied himself an amateur psychopharmacologist. As a small boy, he used to tell his mother that he wanted to grow up to be a drugstore pharmacist in a quaint New England town where the sidewalks were swept clean every morning. He and his mother would live there at peace amid orange maple trees and tidy sparrows. Harley's days would be spent dispensing Valium to a cadre of little old ladies in blue smocks he employed at his drugstore, who would in turn give the Valium to the town's fine and noble citizens, so they might continue to lead their fine and noble lives relatively free from anxiety. But this was really his mother's dream, and when Harley repeated it, he was usually just trying to get himself out of trouble. The only brain chemistry Harley was truly interested in altering was his own.

When Philo was six years old, Harley discovered the chemical compound for Blissful Living Love-Radiance of Infinite Divine Being. Deep in his lair of moldy test tubes, bongs, stale beer, psychedelic fungi, ageless Twinkies, and stainless steel gynecology instruments, Harley could be found every Tuesday heating the new compound with the blue flame of a blowtorch under a customized fishbowl designed to catch the fumes.

On one such Tuesday, Calliope interrupted Harley's labors with a shout to him from outside the shed:

"Harley? Can you go into town and get us some Ajax?"

Harley reached for the stereo and turned down the volume on Jimi Hendrix's *Electric Ladyland* album. "What'd you say?" he shouted back.

"*Ajax!* I need you to go into town and get some Ajax!"

"Yeah, okay… just a minute."

Harley took off his tie-dyed lab smock and his orange-tinted swimming goggles. Science would have to wait. Just before he left the lab, he stooped and stuck his head up into the fume-befogged fishbowl, inhaling deeply.

Calliope and Philo were standing outside at the fence feeding green weeds to the zebras when they heard a loud and particularly joyous *cock-a-doodle-doo!* erupt from Harley inside the shed.

"Oh crap…" Calliope said.

An unfortunate side effect of Blissful Living Love-Radiance of Infinite Divine Being was that it often turned people into roosters.

Calliope squatted next to Philo and gave him a hug. Looking grim, she said, "Daddy's turned himself into a rooster again. We have to go into town with him so he doesn't hurt himself."

"Can't I stay here with the zebras?" Philo didn't like going into town. The people there pinched his cheeks and tousled his blonde hair and told him how cute he was and what a big boy he was becoming. They were patronizing him, and he knew it.

Harley appeared in the doorway of the shed and said, "I'm *'cluck'* fine."

Calliope went over to him and grabbed Harley's cheeks. "Look at me," she said, searching his eyes—not angry, just concerned.

"I'm fine," he repeated. "Fine, *'cluck'*…."

Calliope stepped back a few paces and looked him over. Harley seemed on the verge of a massive rooster attack. His elbows were quivering. The saggy flesh of his neck was twitching.

"I don't like this," Calliope said. "I didn't get married just so you could be a barnyard animal full-time."

"Peace, baby." Harley made a peace sign and strutted across the yard, thrusting his head to and fro and flapping his cocked elbows like Mick Jagger on a bad night.

Making a valiant effort to restrain his *'clucks,'* Harley climbed into the old school bus that he and Calliope used as their primary mode of transportation. The school bus was painted in Day-Glo colors. Its back end had a mural painted on it depicting six Picasso-like sea monsters staring at a naked woman's bulbous behind. People could tell the woman was French because she wore pearls and smoked *Gauloises* from a long black cigarette holder.

The school bus's engine fired right up. Harley waved goodbye to his little family as the bus headed off down the driveway.

"Bye, Daddy!" Philo shouted after him. "Bring us home some Milk Duds for the zebras!"

"Damnit, Harley," Calliope shouted with more of an edge, "you be careful!"

Harley drove along the dirt road leading away from his happy hippie homestead with a walloping dose of Blissful Living Love-Radiance of Infinite Divine Being leaping in his arteries. The world seemed young, vibrant, and alive with sexy goodness. The creek running through his property was giving him a hard-on! He felt like making love to a tree! He wanted to find a mossy knothole in the trunk of some slender maple and just ram it in there—be at one with the sap rising to the leaves.

God! he was in love with everybody! And *Holy Fuck!* he wanted to get it on with everything!

Calliope and Philo watched as the school bus swerved wildly and Harley, stripped to the waist, managed to hang half of his long body out the driver's side window.

"*COCK-A-DOODLE-DOO!*" he crowed. He bobbed once, twice, then three times, like a spastic rooster.

It occurred to Calliope that Harley was probably unfit to drive.

Then the school bus ran off the road and went down an embankment to the right. The bus tilted, went up on two wheels, and crashed on its side. The noise it made was horrible, like a thousand tombstones smashing through a thousand stained glass windows.

Philo and Calliope went running.

Harley, unharmed, crawled out of the wreckage through the school bus's broken windshield. He scalded his left elbow in the steam hissing from the demolished radiator, but that was of little concern. He had more important, more roostery things in mind.

When his distraught family reached him, they found Harley bent over at the waist with his nose deep in the loamy soil, pecking for worms.

2

CALLIOPE, HER TRIAL BY HAMSTERS

Calliope wanted a normal life. She knew normal was an illusion, but she wanted to shoot for it, anyway. She didn't like the idea of Philo flying around on a kite and emulating zeppelins before he could even walk. It wasn't right, damnit. She finally made up her mind and put a stop to it. She wasn't so hot on Harley experimenting with weird chemicals and turning himself into a rooster every Tuesday, either—but she hadn't put her foot down about that one yet, because the sex on Tuesdays was really, *really* great.

I'm such a wimp, Calliope often thought to herself. If she could just stop being so tolerant of weirdness in its early stages, maybe she would stop blaming herself later when things got out of hand.

For instance, she couldn't help thinking it was somehow her fault that Philo's childhood had been marred by exploding hamsters.

The hamster tragedy had its beginnings on Philo's seventh birthday. Calliope had organized a big party for him, inviting over a dozen of his little friends and their parents. Harley's mother had been there, making sour faces at the vegetarian canapés. And Charlene's fat, balding, alcoholic brother, Balmeister, had shown up, too—along with his equally alcoholic wife, Virginia.

"Aunt Virginia! And Uncle Balmeister!" Calliope said in mock-delight, greeting them at the door. "We weren't expecting you!"

"What, you think we'd miss out on our favorite nephew's seventh birthday?" Virginia crowed in a voice ravaged by gin and cigarettes. "Not on your life, Sweetie!"

"Where is that little tiger?!" Balmeister belched, doing a little football tackle dance on the doorstep. Philo ran right over. His Uncle Balmeister hoisted him into the air, saying, *"Hey, hey, hey! Atta boy!* Have I got a surprise for you!"

"What is it?" Philo wanted to know.

"Well, let's go see...."

Balmeister lugged Philo into the kitchen and sat him on the counter. Philo's Aunt Virginia set a large, gift-wrapped package next to him. Philo tore off the wrapping to reveal three hamsters in a gleaming cage.

"Wow! Furry things in a cage!" Philo was astonished.

"They're hamsters, honey!" said Virginia. Then she bent over and coughed. It sounded like she was hawking up a quart of mucus.

("If hippopotamuses could cough," Harley had once said, "they'd cough like Aunt Virginia.")

Calliope quickly took Balmeister aside. "Bal," she whispered, "I don't think the hamsters are such a great idea. I've got a thing about caged animals. I mean, I won't even take Philo to the zoo."

"Oh now Calliope...." Balmeister looked at her as if she was a grey-haired spinster railing against the imagined improprieties of wholesome, Huck Finn-ish youngsters.

"Really, Bal, I don't want Philo growing up thinking it's okay to put animals in cages."

Charlene overheard her. "Oh, for the love of Pete, Calliope," she said. "They're just hamsters."

Calliope's first impulse was to shout, "Shut your trap, you sadistic old hag! You wanted to cage your own son!" But then she thought better of it. Maybe she was making too much of a fuss over the hamsters, after all.

The hamster cage assumed a place of honor on the bookcase in the living room. Philo named the hamsters Manny, Moe, and Jack.

Over the next few weeks, Calliope's initial misgivings about the hamsters proved to be well founded. For hours on end, the hamsters would clutch the cage's bars in their tiny hamster paws. They stared off into the distance with tiny, tensed-up hamster jaw muscles.

Moe was the first to exhibit manic-depressive tendencies. He turned hostile and insane one evening, lunging at fingers and shredding all the newspapers on the bottom of the cage. Then he ran and ran on the little exercise wheel until he exploded in a flash of spontaneous combustion.

The whole family was in the room when Moe detonated. Philo rushed over to the smoking cage. *"What happened?* Where's Moe?"

"Wow. *Far out…*" said Harley as he scrutinized the glowing hamster embers on the exercise wheel. He inhaled a big lungful of hamster smoke and held it.

Calliope whacked him on the side of the head. "Breathe that out," she said. "You don't know where that hamster's been."

"Is Moe dead?" asked Philo.

"Yes, honey." Calliope's tone was gentle. "Moe's soul is probably in your father's lungs at this very moment." She slapped Harley across the back, hard. "Cough it out, damnit!"

Harley blew out a greenish-gray cloud of smoke. *"Whoa… what a rush!"* He paused to find the calm at the center of his being. "Moe's traveling the Hamster Bardo and doing well. I can feel it."

As Harley dabbed at his reddened, watery eyes, Philo whispered, "Go toward the light, Moe. *Go….*"

Calliope told Harley he wasn't allowed to read the *Tibetan Book of the Dead* to Philo as a bedtime story anymore.

□ □ □ □ □ □ □ □ □

Manny was the next to go. He sat in a corner of the cage for days, thinking morbid hamster thoughts. He occasionally watched a TV game show or absent-mindedly chewed on his toenails. Then, with a sudden burst of energy he, too, ran and ran on the exercise wheel until he exploded.

"Philo, keep your father away from that cage," Calliope shouted from the kitchen.

□ □ □ □ □ □ □ □ □

Calliope begged Harley to set the last hamster free. She only relented when Harley pointed out that it was a dry season and they couldn't risk a hamster-related brushfire.

Fearing for Jack's safety, Philo began reading up on hamster psychology. The literature was scant, but in a few weeks he had his answer:

Hamster Lithium.

Philo and his father labored long and hard in the hog shed laboratory to extract lithium salt from raw mineral compounds. They shared many bonding father-to-son conversations. Calliope heard snatches of those conversations when she brought them cheese sandwiches:

"Dad, can frogs be neurotic?"

"Well, son, if they don't successfully navigate Oedipal conflict when they're pollywogs, I guess they could be."

"Oh."

"Pass the dimethyl sulfoxide."

"You betcha."

In the end, Jack was saved.

□ □ □ □ □ □ □ □ □

Hearing of Philo's psychopharmaceutical success with hamsters, the townspeople of Pine Bluff came to him when their zebras had schizophrenic episodes.

Raising zebras had become fashionable in Pine Bluff soon after Calliope and Harley had started doing it. Zebras seemed much more interesting than horses. However, zebras were also more prone to neuroses than their horse counterparts.

Those neuroses stemmed from the fact that all zebras are philosophers. They spend their entire lives wondering if they have black stripes on white, white stripes on black—or maybe the whole damned world is striped, and they're not.

Certain zebras, under the stress of their rigorous metaphysics, broke down and started seeing killer butterflies. Philo sought to rid them of their hallucinations with Zebra Thorazine. And that was how he came to be known as the Psychopharmacologist to All the Creatures, Great and Small.

Calliope was thrilled. Her son was a hero. But she would always feel a twinge of remorse—a vague questioning of her competence as a mother—whenever she thought about those exploding hamsters.

3

HARLEY, HIS ARBOREAL EXILE

When Harley wasn't boldly going where no psycho-pharmacologist had gone before, he liked to pass the time by reading obscure European novels. It was the combination of these two forms of recreation that eventually got him into trouble with his family.

For years, Harley had tinkered with the basic formula of Blissful Living Love-Radiance of Infinite Divine Being. He hoped to eliminate the undesirable side effects—specifically, the part about turning into a rooster. He didn't so much mind the constant hard-on for trees.

One day he introduced an extract of mistletoe to the formula. The result was a potent new cure for AIDS, but since Harley was HIV-negative, that breakthrough went undiscovered. He ingested his usual Tuesday dose of the drug and sat back to wait for it to kick in. To help pass the time, he picked up a paperback copy of Italo Calvino's *The Baron in the Trees*.

As the Blissful Living Love-Radiance of Infinite Divine Being came on, Harley found himself mesmerized by Calvino's book. It was the story of Cosimo, a pre-adolescent Italian nobleman of the 18th-century who rebelled against his parents by climbing into the trees, where he stayed for the rest of his life. Cosimo hunted, sowed crops, pruned orchards, fought forest fires—even managed to have love affairs—all without ever setting foot on the ground again. His tale made life in the trees seem more noble, more passionate and meaningful, than any comparable life on earth.

Harley, reading, thought to himself, *I could be this guy!*

Filled with new purpose, he cast the book aside and gathered up his tree climbing gear.

That was a few months before Philo's thirteenth birthday. Harley had been up in the trees ever since.

Philo reacted to his father's absence in a number of peculiar ways. For a while, he plodded through the woods with a bucket and a housepainter's brush, smearing a special mixture of mashed bananas and motor oil on the branches of Harley's favorite trees. Philo's plan was to get his dad to slip and break a kneecap, thereby rendering him earthbound again. *A father with busted-up kneecaps was better than no father at all,* he reasoned. Harley, however, had an uncanny knack for avoiding greased branches, and the only result of Philo's labors throughout that long first spring and summer was a slight dip in the growth curve of the local aphid population.

In the fall, Philo started getting into trouble at school. He wore a black cape, carried a loaded water pistol, and walked to his classes with a limp. He used the royal "we" when referring to himself, as in:

"We should like to expel our urates, please," when he raised his hand to go to the restroom.

"We found our instrument emitting a spontaneous mating cry, aroused by the bassoon," when asked to stop making elephant noises on his French horn.

"We would sooner play Twister naked in the presence of a dozen bellicose wolverines," when summoned to the blackboard to solve an algebra problem.

His teachers began to complain about this irksome behavior, sending reports home to Calliope studded with phrases like, "Philo's willful eccentricities are costing him his grade in History," and "his antics, however amusing, are distracting to the rest of the class." Philo, when confronted by his mother with these reports, merely shrugged, then beat his hands against his chest like a mountain gorilla to the accompaniment of a terrible ululating hooting that raised the hair on the back of Calliope's neck. She understood the act was meant as a parody of Harley.

Philo wanted his father out of the trees.

Finally, Calliope climbed a sturdy maple tree to confer with Harley about Philo's behavior. Harley flatly refused to leave the safety of his leafy bowers for a series of parent-teacher conferences. He wouldn't give her a plausible explanation why. Calliope made several eloquent entreaties on behalf of their son's mental health. Harley wouldn't budge—but together they hit upon the idea of bribing Philo by giving him a motorcycle.

"If I find you a motorcycle, will you stop all this 'we' crap?" Harley asked Philo from the boughs of Brautigan's Oak, where they met every Saturday.

"We will, indeed, stop all the 'we' excrement," Philo agreed.

"And no more gorilla hoots? They scare your mother."

Philo nodded in the affirmative.

"Okay then."

"We always find it most edifying to chat with you, sir."

"Oh… and one more thing. Lose the cape."

"As you wish, Father."

Philo limped eastward.

So that's how Philo came into possession of a hellish black and chrome 1953 Vincent Black Shadow—the motorcycle of his dreams. As soon as he learned to ride it, his behavior became almost normal, spiked only by occasional incidents of eccentricity that were more glandular than willful in their origin.

He wanted, more than anything, to gobble a handful of Rabbit Mescaline and make violent love to the girls' P.E. coach—Miss Randi Lafontaine—on the seat of the Vincent as it screamed along the open highway at 120 mph. He practiced shifting with his pants off in the woods behind the hog sheds, constantly afraid his father would catch him at it and have him institutionalized.

"But my dad lives in the damn trees!" Philo imagined yelping as he was forced into a straightjacket.

"At least he's not naked as a jaybird. At least he doesn't touch himself there," said the men in white coats as they hauled him away.

Philo's fantasy about the girls' P.E. coach came to an abrupt and intimidating end when he found out that Miss Lafontaine was living with a former Pine Bluff High School varsity squad linebacker whose monstrous genitalia had earned him the locker room nickname *Slinky*.

4

MRS. ANDERSEN, HER CARNIVOROUS CHICKENS

Mrs. Andersen was the Marndog family's closest neighbor. She lived a few miles down the road in an old farmhouse that the tourists were always taking pictures of because it was so very darn picturesque. She raised chickens there and watched a lot of television.

She was almost a hundred years old and fat, but that didn't slow her down much. Her clothes made her look like a rogue sofa humping around in search of some cozy living room to occupy. Her face had the spongy, caved-in appearance of a jack-o'-lantern that had been left out in the sun too long. She was Pine Bluff's oldest resident and beloved by just about everyone.

The years had taken their toll on Mrs. Andersen's mind, however. It would have shocked her in her sixties to find out how lush and perverse her imagination would become in her nineties. Almost the entire history of Pine Bluff was mixed up in there with her own personal history and a whole lifetime of secret grudges and fantasies.

Feeding the chickens, Mrs. Andersen thought back to the day when frogs rained from the skies above Pine Bluff's Main Street. That had been Captain Nitt-Witt's doing. He was old now, almost her age. When was the last time she'd seen him? *Ten years ago? Twenty?* He was out in front of Old Camozzi's Saloon wearing nothing but a ratty old red bathrobe. She remembered seeing his penis—a chubby white worm drooping from the tangled bird's nest of his crotch. He was shaking it at the tourists—jostling the normal scheme of things.

She was surprised God didn't squash him like a bug. Why America put up with rebels like Captain Nitt-Witt, she didn't understand. At least you never saw that kind of horseplay on *Wheel of Fortune*. Shameless money-grubbing and the right to own patio furniture—that was what made America strong.

Shaking her gray head in disapproval, Mrs. Andersen thought of the many women who'd offered their bodies to the Captain up at Nitt-Witt Ridge. She didn't believe that ugly talk about a Catholic nun dying from ecstasy under the pounding of his love. But she had talked to some of the others—women in their forties who should have known better. They said he had the stamina of a racehorse, even though he was well into his seventies by then. She especially pitied the younger women, the thrill-seekers up from the universities. She wondered if the Captain somehow juiced their youth—if his seed made them old before their time.

A chicken pecked Mrs. Andersen on her leg, shocking her out of her reveries. *Ouch!* Her chickens were her pets. They'd never shown her any hostility before. And something else was odd. The chickens weren't going after their feed.

First Oswald, her owl, gets plugged up—and now this.

She decided to call the Marndog boy. He had more sass than any teenager she'd ever run across, but he seemed to have a way with animals.

Philo was riding his beloved clanking, clattering black and chrome motorcycle around in tight circles on the dirt driveway in front of his house, dreaming of the day when he would turn sixteen. He would get his license then and be able to ride out on the open highway, straight into the sun. He would also be of legal age to wreck school buses, just like his father.

He could hardly wait.

Calliope appeared on the porch with a cordless telephone pressed to her ear. "Philo!" she called out, waving to him. He pulled up beside her and let the motorcycle idle. "Mrs. Andersen's on the phone. Her owl's constipated."

"Tell her to feed it some prunes."

"She wants to know if you can come take a look at it."

"I'm a psychopharmacologist. My job description doesn't say anything about poking a flashlight up some dumb bird's butt."

"She also thinks her chickens might be turning into sociopaths."

"Aw, Ma!"

"C'mon, Philo… do it for me." Calliope pulled down on the hem of her dress and got a sad clown look on her face. "If you spent some more time around chickens, maybe you could figure out how to get your father down out of the trees."

Philo revved the Vincent Black Shadow's engine. "This sucks, mom."

"I know, honey…." There was that sad clown look again.

Philo thought his mother might be making fun of him, but he wasn't sure. He gunned the Vincent, did an ungraceful wheelie, and then he roared off down the driveway in a heroic cloud of dust. If he had to go all the way to Mrs. Andersen's house, there was no way in hell he was walking.

"I don't know what's wrong…" Mrs. Andersen said when Philo got there. She was wringing her flabby hands as she led him to the henhouse. "They're off their feed and they seem downright mean."

Philo looked through the henhouse door onto a sea of haughty chickens. He went inside and climbed up on a low, crusty rail to peer into a hen's nest. "They look healthy enough," Philo said. "Not constipated, are they?"

"No. Just the opposite."

Philo slipped off the rail and landed thigh-deep in an enormous feathered mound of chicken shit. It had an awful ammonia smell. He had an impulse to plunge his hand deep into the green-and-white slime, as a tactile experiment, but then he thought better of it.

"Do you want some cookies?" Mrs. Andersen asked him.

"Yeah, *right*.... I'm up to my ass in chicken shit here, Mrs. Andersen. You got a beer?"

"Philo! You're too young to drink."

Philo made a face like a scolding old woman. He could take all the Zebra Thorazine or bovine anti-depressants that he wanted, but he still couldn't get a beer. Not even a warm Budweiser. All adults were raving, hysterical hypocrites.

Oh well... what could he do about it? *Nothing*. Philo climbed back up on the rail and peered into another hen's nest. Much to his chagrin, he found a bloody dead bulldog in there sprinkled with hen feathers.

"Oh, man! They've got a dead dog up here."

Mrs. Andersen perked right up. "Ernest? Is that Ernest?"

"What's left of him...."

"I thought he ran away."

Philo shook his head. "Nope. These goddamn chickens are meat-eaters." He reached up to investigate the nest above him, a rounded thatch of straw that could have been home to several large buzzards. As he tipped the nest's edge, a board squeaked, and then a half-eaten bear carcass toppled out onto his face.

Philo lost his cool and shrieked just like a girl. *"A bear! They killed a frickin' bear!"*

The chickens clucked furiously.

"Oh my..." Mrs. Andersen said.

5

PHILO, HIS SURLY STONE SKIPPING

After submitting to Mrs. Andersen's garden hose to wash all the bear gore and chicken shit off his person, Philo entered the woods to look for his father. He was perplexed by the chickens' symptoms, unsure as to how he might medicate them. He was hoping Harley would have some answers.

"Hey Dad! Are you out there?" shouted Philo, parking his motorcycle beneath Brautigan's Oak. He cupped his hands to direct his shout out beyond the tree's gigantic limbs. *"Dad! I need to talk to you!"*

There was a rustling on the forest wind. Far off in the distance, Harley appeared at the top of an enormous elm, waving his arms and crowing a faint *"cock-a-doodle-doo!"* A blue tree climber's rope cast out in front of him like a thread.

Philo had seen his father move through the forest trees many times before, but he still found it thrilling. Harley seemed to possess the combined skills and grace of Tarzan, Spiderman, and an absurdly large breed of flying squirrel. He swiftly moved along hidden paths from elm to pine to oak. Twigs and branches bent to help him on his way. His leaps were stupendous, his agility astonishing. Smug *'clucks'* of satisfaction escaped him whenever he performed some tricky maneuver particularly well.

Within minutes, he was reaching down to help Philo up into Brautigan's Oak. They sat together on a limb, swinging their feet.

"Philo, what's up? How's your mom?"

"She's fine. She just wishes you weren't living in these damn trees."

"She doesn't understand my 'cluck' Oneness with nature."

"Yeah, well, you know mom…."

"Feisty."

"Yeah."

Recently, Philo had been obsessed with trying to catch a glimpse of his mother naked. His own mother! Hormones were running amok in his system, making him stew in the bubbling grease of his own sensuality. The other day he'd been so exquisitely horny that he'd turned a somersault in the bathtub, trying to suck himself. He worried that he would grow up to be a solitary homo.

But could he tell his father this?

No. There was no sense in getting Tarzan worked up about onanism and Oedipal rivalry.

"Dad," Philo began cautiously, "Mrs. Andersen's chickens have started killing things."

"What sort of thing? 'cluck?'"

"Bears, bulldogs—I don't know what else."

"She's been letting those chickens watch television again, hasn't she?"

"I don't know, dad… it's weird. I can't figure it out."

"Sounds to me like some sort of mass chicken psychosis. You're dealing with a 'cluck' mob mentality here."

"What do you expect with chickens? They don't read Nietzsche or Camus."

Harley thought for a moment and then he patted his son on the back. "I think I've got something that'll help you out," he said. "Meet me back here tomorrow."

Without a trace of sissiness or self-doubt, Harley leapt up and scampered along a limb, back toward the forest.

"Hey, uh, dad?" Philo called after him.

Harley turned around. "Yeah, Philo…?"

"Sometimes mom, y'know… well, we both kind of wonder if…."

"I'll come home? 'cluck?'"

Philo thought he saw a look of scorn on his father's face. He decided to be strong, to not press the issue, although he wanted his father to come more than he had ever wanted anything—even a Vincent Black Shadow.

"Forget it," Philo said. "It's stupid. We all do what we have to do, right? I'll see you tomorrow."

"Someday I hope you'll understand, Philo. Until then, tell your mom I love her. You, too. Peace, *'cluck.'* Be free...."

Harley hurried off into the awaiting limbs of the forest with a joyous *"Cock-a-doodle-doo!"*

Philo just sat there, kicking at a twig. "Peace, *'cluck.'* Be free...." He hawked up a gob of sarcasm: "Yeah, right."

The world was far more screwed-up than Philo thought should be allowed. Chickens were not supposed to kill bears. Fathers were not supposed to live in trees. *And mothers,* he thought with extreme self-loathing, *were not supposed to seem sexy to their sons!*

He was wrong about that last assumption, of course. But Philo had yet to get around to more than a cursory reading of Freud.

Philo hiked through the woods, thinking these things without paying attention to where he was going. He ended up at Gargoyle Creek.

The trees along the creek's banks were knobby and gnarled, thrust up from the soil like the hands of gigantic demons. Their branches grew so close together that they blotted out the sun. Spanning the creek itself was a bridge of twisted tree roots arching across a smallish waterfall. A gigantic stone gargoyle—the creek's namesake—squatted in a shallow pool upstream like some belly-bloated Buddha. Damp clumps of ferns, moss, and weird mushrooms sprouted everywhere in abundance.

Philo walked to the center of the bridge and started skipping stones at the gargoyle. *Click!* went a stone as it nicked the gargoyle's belly.

Local legend had it that Captain Nitt-Witt had carved the gargoyle from one big serpentine boulder in the autumn of 1942. Some people thought the gargoyle was sitting on the entrance to a secret passageway that led all the way up to Nitt-Witt Ridge. They claimed the Captain had dug the passageway so he could hide his opium-smoking Japanese fishmonger friends from the people who wanted to put them into concentration camps during World War II.

Splish, splish, splish—click! Another stone hit the gargoyle's belly.

Philo thought all that Captain Nitt-Witt stuff was just bullshit.

So some old guy had built a weird castle out of abalone shells and beer cans up on Nitt-Witt Ridge. That didn't make him a legend, a goddamn folk hero, for chrissake....

Anyway, there were other stories, too. About how he killed a nun, for instance... or how he liked to shake his pecker at blue-haired old ladies on Main Street. When all the stories were added up, Captain Nitt-Witt sounded more like a cranky old fart with mild schizoid tendencies, rather than some stealthy saint who went around practicing secular humanism on everybody before it was considered fashionable.

Still, what he'd done was kind of cool.... He might have been fun to have as a father. Philo thought about what it would be like if Harley was out of the trees and instead they were building a castle together, or saving a bunch of Japanese guys with a secret tunnel.

Yeah, Philo decided, *Captain Nitt-Witt would've made a totally great dad....*

Splish—click!

Philo was out of rocks. He was about to go off to look for more when a large raccoon padded down to the edge of the creek and reared up on its hindquarters to show him a mystery.

The raccoon was wearing red overalls.

It was a strange and startling vision, but Philo retained some humor about the situation. He decided to pay the raccoon a compliment. "Nice overalls there, little dude," he said.

The raccoon stuck its thumbs under the straps of the overalls and tugged—a small gesture of raccoonish pride. Then it leaned down for a quick drink from the creek and scampered away.

As he watched the raccoon's red rump disappear into the woods, Philo said to himself, "Jeez, I must be trippin'." His father had informed him about hallucinations. A raccoon in red overalls would certainly qualify as one. He suspected there might be some unusual neurochemical reaction brewing inside his brain. *Was his serotonin level unusually high? Were his dopamine receptors blocked?*

"There's more weirdness in heaven and earth than you can shake a stick at, Philo…."

Philo's ears tried to leap off either side of his skull. He took a sharp intake of air and whirled in the direction of the gruff old voice. An old man was standing beside him on the bridge.

The old man was tugging at a clot of hair in his long Rip Van Winkle beard. He was only wearing high top tennis shoes and a ratty red bathrobe. Philo guessed him to be at least a hundred, if not older. The wrinkles in his forehead were deep enough to hide nickels. He had a bulbous, pockmarked turnip of a nose. He bold blue eyes were still young and alive with a bad boy's twinkle, but the rest of him was old, *old, OLD*….

"Who're you?" Philo's heart felt like a hummingbird stuck in the cage of his lungs.

The old man was sublimely serene. He yawned, and then spat a wad of tobacco juice into the stream. "You know me," he said.

"The hell I do."

"Everyone knows me in these parts. Or at least they know my home."

"What home?"

"Nitt-Witt Ridge."

Philo's anxiety was replaced by feelings of awe and wonder that verged on a bewildered kind of love. "You're Captain Nitt-Witt?"

The old man bowed graciously. "Alias Doctor Tinkerpaw. At your service."

"Everyone thinks you're dead."

"Not dead. Just resting. I don't get out as much as I used to."

Philo still thought he might be hallucinating. "Nobody's seen you around since the sixties," he said.

"You did. Way back one Halloween, about seven years ago."

"I don't remember that."

"I didn't want you to." Captain Nitt-Witt put his big knuckled hands on Philo's shoulders and grinned. "It was just before your seventh birthday, when all those hamsters were exploding."

"I remember that."

"I taught you how to fly...."

Philo felt like he was in the company of an ace hypnotist. His eyelids were getting heavy. He was becoming very, very sleepy.

6

CAPTAIN NITT-WITT, HIS HOME AND GARDEN TOUR

He was just a first grader in a pirate costume, but in his mind he was a swarthy swashbuckler.

When Philo was six years old the whole world was alive and mysterious and monsters were something real that could bite your head off. His friends were mostly in the first grade just like he was and they all ran around like maniacs playing tag at night in fields of wet summer grass that came up past their elbows. What made the game more interesting was that they knew they might run into goblins out there.

Philo wanted to be a pirate when he grew up, so on his sixth Halloween he was one. His mother made him some pants out of an old satin nightie and wrapped some scarves around his head and put a gold clip-on earring on his ear and she even found an eyepatch for his eye to wear.

Philo knew that when he got older he'd be the kind of pirate who licked women's boobies and made men walk the plank. He'd have lots of gold and cannons and a parrot on his shoulder that said bad words in French. When someone said his name—Captain Philo!—people would get so scared they'd pee in their pants, even if they had an important meeting to go to right then.

He'd be the terror of at least seven or eight different seas.

Halloween was a special time for kids like him. You got to run around all night trying to break peoples' eardrums shouting "Trick-or-treat!" You could blow up the mailboxes of people you didn't like and throw lawn chairs in their fishponds and leave burning sacks of dog crap on their doorsteps. On other nights you could get in big trouble for doing that stuff, but on Halloween it was okay. That was the rule.

Also, when you got tired of all that running around, you and some of your other best friends could get together and tell ghost stories and break into a haunted house.

There were two haunted houses in Pine Bluff. One was the place where the sexy Irish-Chinese lady lived who everybody thought was a vampire. The other was Nitt-Witt Ridge.

On his sixth Halloween, Philo and some of his friends decided to break into Nitt-Witt Ridge. The year before they had tried breaking into the Irish-Chinese vampire lady's house, but she was just too scary. She had chopsticks for fangs and she stuck firecrackers down your pants before she sucked your blood. All of her victims had been found with burned up underpants and a four-leaf clover stuck in their nose. The police couldn't prove anything, but they knew it was her.

Everybody was standing on the bridge across Gargoyle Creek just before they decided. Jimmy Marrsden, dressed like Batman, was telling a long weird story about Captain Nitt-Witt, about how he got so old that even the worms wouldn't eat him, so he had to be a ghost forever. "...and that's why Nitt-Witt Ridge is haunted," Jimmy said in a spooky voice. "The ghost of Captain Nitt-Witt walks around there with a pack of devil dogs."

Dan Fleabutt—that was his real name!—was so scared he was almost crying under his skinny ghost costume. "My dad saw him! He said his beard was full of blood."

Jimmy looked at Fleabutt and said, even spookier, "They say he went crazy and killed a nun."

"And ate her," said Kent Huckaby. Then he laughed.

Kent was fat. He had on a fat ghost costume. It took a lot to get him scared.

Fleabutt started crying. He was such a baby.

Philo skipped a stone at the gargoyle in the creek. Two girls were with them on the bridge—Lisa Markham and her friend, Mickelodia—and he was trying to show off by acting bored.

Jimmy shouted, "I saw the gargoyle move! Let's get out of here!"

Philo was pretty sure Jimmy was faking, so he stayed where he was, but the girls screamed like they were really afraid and everybody ran away into the forest.

The gargoyle looked even scarier after Philo was left by himself. It was like some big ugly dragon-monkey with fangs and claws and big ugly bat wings. It had a potbelly, too. His mom said his dad would get one of those if he didn't stop drinking beer. But his dad wasn't fat or afraid of anything—he climbed trees and knew karate—and Philo wished he with him right then.

"Be brave, Philo," his dad always said when there was a green octopus-monster under the bed or a blue man with sparks coming out of his head in the closet. So Philo tried to be brave. He skipped another rock at the gargoyle.

The gargoyle moved! Its claws were stretching out at him!

Philo ran to catch up with the others.

It was easy to find them. The girls were still screaming, only now they were doing it just for fun, giggling between screams. Everybody ran out from under the trees into an open field. The stars were so bright they made the grass look silver like an ocean. The moon was shining down big and orange from over a mountain up ahead. On top of the mountain, Philo saw the shadow of a crazy castle.

"Look! Nitt-Witt Ridge!" Lisa Markham said from behind her green mummy mask. She had a cold, so it came out sounding funny. She talked like she really was that mummy.

Mickelodia came up next to Philo and held his hand. It gave him a funny feeling in his chest, like he had too much air. "It's beautiful," Mickelodia said, staring up at the castle. "I've never seen it in the moonlight before."

Mickelodia was dressed like a fairy princess. She had a fancy wand and long red hair and a sparkling silver crown on her head. Philo thought she was kind of beautiful. She also smelled good. Holding her hand made him nervous, though. He hoped Kent and Jimmy wouldn't see it and start making fun of him.

"I dare anyone to go up there," Jimmy said.

"I double-dare you, peckerhead," Kent said.

"I double-double-dare you, fartsucker."

Mickelodia squeezed Philo's hand really tight and said to him, "I'll do it if you do it."

Philo's stomach flopped. He didn't want to go up there, but now he had to. Everyone else was going "Oooooohhhh!" and saying in Mickelodia's voice, really high, "C'mon, Philo, I'll do it if you do it." He couldn't say no and act like he was more afraid than some girl. He'd be called a chicken for the rest of his life.

"Sure," he said, trying to sound brave, "let's all do it."

"You're crazy," Fleabutt said.

"No way," Kent said.

"C'mon," Philo said, "don't be babies." He felt better now that Kent was the one acting chicken.

"You go first then," Jimmy told Philo.

"Okay, but you guys have to follow me."

"Don't worry, pissbrains… we'll follow you."

Mickelodia was all excited. "Let's go!" she shouted.

So they started up the mountain. Nobody else talked, except for Lisa Markham, who said in her teeny-weeny mummy voice:

"Guys, I'm scared."

Philo climbed up the mountain, followed by Mickelodia and Lisa Markham and then Jimmy and Kent and Dan Fleabutt—who were all trying to look up Mickelodia's skirt. Philo held Mickelodia and Lisa's hands to help them over the steeper parts. When they got to the top, they were standing right in front of Captain Nitt-Witt's famous house: Nitt-Witt Ridge.

"Wow," Philo said. It was about all he could think of to say.

"Neato," said Dan Fleabutt.

Nitt-Witt Ridge was a huge castle built out of junk. It had crazy, zigzagging walls made from beer cans and abalone shells and hubcaps and broken TV sets. It even had some toilet seats for windows. A big deer stared at them from the garden, eating roses. Strange creaky weathervanes pointed up at the stars from the arches above the abalone shell staircases.

A gigantic orange moon was rising right behind the roof, making everything glow. Fireflies sparked in the shadows under trees and somewhere a fountain was splashing in the dark. Everyone just stood there staring, feeling like they were in a fairy tale.

Mickelodia hugged Philo from behind and whispered: "Philo, have you ever been up here before?"

"No. Have you?"

"No! I can't believe he built this whole place all by himself."

"It must've took him forever."

A twisted iron gate banged open and shut in the wind. Jimmy Marrsden pointed to it and said, "I dare anybody to go in there."

"No way," Dan Fleabutt said.

"Devil dogs," Lisa Markham wheezed from behind her mummy mask.

"Nun's guts," said Kent Huckaby.

A wolf howled someplace far away, sending chills like frozen lizards crawling up their spines. Suddenly, Captain Nitt-Witt was out on an abalone shell balcony with the moon above his head.

"Hey down there! Why don't you come on up!" he shouted in his grumpy old man's voice. "Trick or Treat!"

He was the oldest old man anyone there had ever seen. His tangled white beard was hanging over a ratty red bathrobe. His long gray hair was matted like the fur on a scraggly opossum.

Everyone screamed and ran away—except for Philo, who stood his ground. Mickelodia hid behind a boulder and shouted to him: "Philo! Come on!"

Philo looked at Mickelodia over his shoulder and waved her away. "No. You go ahead." He wasn't sure why, but he didn't want to run away.

Mickelodia disappeared over the side of the mountain with the others. Philo stared up at Captain Nitt-Witt, trying to look brave.

"I'm not afraid of you," Philo said.

Captain Nitt-Witt laughed. "Yes, you are—but you've got guts, kid."

Philo pretended he was a pirate and stared even harder at Captain Nitt-Witt, trying not to blink. He was just a first grader, but he wanted to look like the toughest first grader there'd ever been. "You're not a ghost," he said.

"Nope, I'm not a ghost," Captain Nitt-Witt agreed. "I'm just an old, old man who's a little touched in the head."

"You built this whole place all by yourself?"

"Yep."

"How'd you do it?"

"Come on up, Philo, and I'll show you."

For the second time that night, Philo's chest felt like it was filled up with too much air. "How do you know my name?" he asked the Captain.

"I know everyone's name. I also know the number of hairs on your head, and I've got a jar of your old toenail clippings on the mantle over my fireplace. Come on up."

Captain Nitt-Witt actually had to go down to the twisted iron gate to get him. Philo was way too confused to find his own way up. He thought he was about to meet an angel, or maybe even God.

"When I started out, I had no more in mind of doing this than I did of growing feathers. But now—" the Captain spun around with his arms held out wide, like he wanted to hug everything around him—"now it's the finest monstrosity this side of hell."

"It's pretty neat here, all right," Philo agreed. He didn't know about understatements yet, but he'd just made one.

He and the Captain were walking through a tiled courtyard lit up with fireflies and Chinese lanterns. The sound of bubbling water was everywhere, spouting from fountains in the shape of mermaids, cherubs, gargoyles, and sea monsters. The fountains were surrounded by orchids, *ferns, and vines of bougainvillea. Tall flowering trees provided a leafy canopy overhead, full of chirping birds. A grizzly bear stood in a dark corner. For just an instant, Philo thought the bear might be alive, but then he saw it was carved from the trunk of a giant redwood.*

Inside Nitt-Witt Ridge, the walls were inlaid with glistening abalone shells. The whole place was lit up with candles and antique hurricane lamps. There were weird stained glass windows in every corner and spotlighted niches here and there showcasing surrealistic paintings. The furniture was made of surf-smoothed burlwood draped with sheepskin covers. Captain Nitt-Witt sat down in a fantastic burlwood throne and started smoking an equally fantastic burlwood pipe while Philo wandered around looking at things.

"What do you want most out of life," Philo?" the Captain asked him.

Philo stood gazing at a tiny scale model of Nitt-Witt Ridge under a sea-turtle-sized crystal dome. The little fountains, no bigger than his pinkie, were actually spouting almost invisible jets of water.

"I want to live here," Philo said.

"That may be possible. But you have to help your parents grow up first. What else do you want?"

"I want to fly like a bird," Philo spread his arms and ran around the room like a bird spiraling on a wind current.

"You're not afraid of the sky?"

"Nope. When I was a baby, I used to fly around on a kite."

Philo halted in front of a painting of a naked woman being fitted for a gown of red feathers. The woman's face was completely hidden by the top of the gown, which looked like the head of an angry red owl. Philo had never seen anything quite like it.

The Captain walked up behind him carrying a heavy tweed overcoat. "Y'like that? My friend Max Ernst painted it. It's called The Robing of the Bride.*"*

"It's weird…. Good weird, I mean."

"Here: put this on." Captain Nitt-Witt held the overcoat open and Philo backed into it while continuing to stare at the painting. The overcoat was absurdly big on him.

"When Max Ernst was a boy about your age, he had a pet cockatoo whose wings were pink as a baby's gums. One day the cockatoo died and young Max knew such grief that he grew up to be a great surrealist painter."

Captain Nitt-Witt opened a burlwood cabinet and removed a sack of owl feathers and a pot of industrial glue.

"This is gonna stink a bit, but just try to ignore it."

The Captain took a brush from the pot and slopped a bright bubbly magenta glob on the back of the overcoat, then sprinkled it with feathers.

Philo kept staring at the painting. The woman's uncovered breasts were lopsided. "What're you doing?" he asked the Captain.

"Teaching you to fly."

"It stinks bad. What is that junk?"

"Owl feathers and a little industrial glue. Hush now…. Look at the painting." Captain Nitt-Witt returned to his story as he proceeded to cover the entire overcoat with glue and feathers.

"Birds were a constant in my friend Max's work. He couldn't keep them out. The children in his paintings were threatened by nightingales. A lot of the naked women he painted had beaks and feathered heads. The secret hero of his books was named Loplop, Superior of the Birds. If you're lucky, you'll meet Loplop tonight."

The Captain stepped back to admire his handiwork. "There! Finished. You look great!"

Philo turned to face him. He looked like an ostrich just returned from a high dive into a pool of strawberry Jell-O, but he was smiling as if he had on his first tuxedo.

"Now flap your arms and whistle like this…" Captain Nitt-Witt whistled a strange bird-like tune and cocked his old elbows like an arthritic penguin.

Philo tried to do the same, flapping his arms as the Captain had instructed.

"No, it's not working. The glue needs to dry or you'll lose all your feathers. Here: take a swig of this…." The Captain produced a bright silver flask from his robe. He unscrewed the top and handed it to Philo.

"What is it?"

Captain Nitt-Witt snorted. "Radish juice and horse piss. Just drink it."

Philo took a swig and made a face. "Yech!"

He stumbled. The Captain grabbed him by his cheeks and guided him to the floor. "Now sit down before you fall down," he said calmly. "You're about to go to sleep."

Philo felt dizzy. The room was melting around him like it was made of wax. Comets were shooting off the furniture and streaking along the ceiling, leaving trails of neon-colored light. Then Captain Nitt-Witt leaned over him, his face a smiling dandelion sun with fireworks spinning around the edges. He opened his mouth full of sparkling minnows and said, "You won't remember this until you're ready."

"Gladula bimba beri snoo…" Philo muttered. He felt his lymph nodes unfurling. He howled and then the Sleep Owl came and turned out all the lights.

Philo woke up on a pool table with a bad taste in his mouth. He still had on the overcoat covered with feathers. It still stunk from all the glue. He rolled over on his side and looked around. He was in a bar—a placed called Old Camozzi's Saloon that he'd only seen from outside on the sidewalk until then. Six-year-olds weren't supposed to go into bars.

There was a sexy lady with an owl head standing next to him, watching him with round golden eyes. She had on tight jeans and a thin T-shirt. Philo knew she was a lady—and sexy—because she had really curvy boobs.

"You must be Loplop," he said. Loplop nodded. They shook hands. "Captain Nitt-Witt said I might see you. You look a little like that lady in the painting… only prettier."

Only your boobies aren't lopsided, *was what Philo was really thinking.*

He sat up. People were staring at him—cowboys and waitresses mostly. Nobody he recognized. Loplop took Philo's hand and helped him *jump down from the pool table. She led him over to the saloon's big double doors and they went out into the night.*

They stopped under a yellow streetlamp on the sidewalk. Loplop came around to stand in front of him. She couldn't talk, but she was flapping her arms and whistling a magic tune. Philo remembered what Captain Nitt-Witt had taught him and he did exactly what Loplop was doing. He almost peed in his pants when they both shot up into the air like rockets.

Philo went soaring above the tiny lights of Pine Bluff. "Wow! COOL!" he shouted. He was flying! The wind was roaring in his ears. He was so excited he was shivering. He didn't know what was holding him up, but he was almost sure he wasn't going to fall.

Loplop led him out over the dark forest that bordered the town. In a moonlit meadow far below them, Mickelodia was walking along in her fairy princess costume. She seemed to be singing to herself. She started to skip, then she jumped and twirled around in a weird kind of fairy princess dance.

Philo swooped down to say hello.

"Mickelodia! Look! I can fly!"

Mickelodia looked up. Philo zoomed down out of the sky, wagging his arms and legs like a spastic frog, trying to get her attention.

Mickelodia twirled herself around and around. She was so happy, it was all she could think to do. "Philo, you can!" she practically sang to him. "You really can *fly!"*

"Yeah!" Philo shouted back at her. He was just about to crash into a tree. When he saw what was about to happen, he pulled his neck in like a scared turtle and grabbed at the air with his hands and feet, but there was nothing to grab onto.

Loplop lunged down out of the sky and took Philo's hand, pulling him up and away. They headed off toward Nitt-Witt Ridge flying faster than ever.

"Philo, I love you!" Mickelodia shouted from behind them.

"What?" Philo couldn't hear her with all the wind rushing in his ears.

"I LOVE YOU!"

After Philo disappeared way off in the night, Mickelodia giggled and hugged herself while she did another twirling dance. Seeing Philo fly was even better than that time she saw a flying saucer when she was four years old. She wondered if anyone would believe her when she told them about it. No one had believed the flying saucer story, but now she was a lot older than four. She was eight.

But maybe even eight wasn't old enough, *she thought as she twirled her way home.*

Philo and Loplop circled Nitt-Witt Ridge like drunken bats. Loplop was teaching him how to follow the wind currents through branches and belfries, how to catch June bugs on the wing, how to put a package of clouds on his back and unburden himself above thirsting plants. Philo was intoxicated with his newfound powers of flight. He felt like Peter Pan—and Nitt-Witt Ridge was his Never-Never Land.

Everything was happening much faster than usual, as if he was remembering something he'd already done before. Chasing a sphinx moth, Philo flew in too low through Nitt-Witt Ridge's courtyard. He skimmed the top of a fountain and soaked his clothes. The shock of the water made him lose his concentration and he tumbled out of control. He would have bashed his head into a concrete wall if Loplop hadn't lunged down from the clouds again. She snatched his collar in her beak, and with a twist of her powerful owl head, wrested him back up toward the stars.

They flew away from the Ridge then, high above the forest. Philo, ever the daredevil, executed a wobbly barrel roll. At the end of it, he lost his bearings and again went tumbling out of control. Loplop saved him with her beak once more.

"Thanks," said Philo. They flew back to Pine Bluff side-by-side.

Together, they soared down the center of Main Street, level with the roofs of the stores. Then a gust of wind picked Philo up and hurled him through the window of a Mexican bakery.

He was just flying along and then BAM!—the next thing he knew he was tumbling against someone's doughnut counter in a hail of glass. He sat up, baffled to find he was unharmed. A cinnamon-sprinkled churro *zonked him on the side of his head, thrown by Captain Nitt-Witt, who stood bouncing on his toes behind the counter wearing a shabby baker's uniform.*

The Captain was looking even more crazed than usual. With his eyes practically bugging out of his skull, he waved another sticky cinnamon bun at Philo and shouted, "Hey there, Icarus! How 'bout a scone!"

"Oh. It's you..." Philo sighed. This all had to be a dream, he told himself. He tried to figure out some way to test it. Maybe if he had to pee really bad, the dream would end. Either that, or he'd wet the bed.

"Can I have some water?" Philo asked. "I'm really thirsty."

Captain Nitt-Witt handed him a glass of water. Philo gulped it down. He'd be waking up any minute now, he was sure of it.

7

PHILO, HIS LEAVE-TAKING

"Remember that sense of freedom you had, up there in the sky?"

"I do now. *Wow.*..." Philo's recollection of his flight with Loplop seven years earlier seemed just as real and vivid as his present situation, standing on the bridge over Gargoyle Creek with Captain Nitt-Witt.

"That's what your father feels when he's up in the trees. It's the reason he won't come down."

"I don't blame him."

"You did right up until now."

Philo had to think about that one. He skipped another stone at the gargoyle.

Sure, when he was younger he'd been mad that his dad was so fucking weird. Even before taking up residence in the trees full-time, Harley had preferred second-story branches to the flat, dull ground. It had made Philo's life difficult. Little League baseball just hadn't been the same for Philo as it had been for the other kids, for example. Most of their fathers sat in the bleachers cheering them on, but where was his dad? Perched way up in a big maple tree just outside the left field foul line.

Harley liked to start up his chainsaw and let it roar each time Philo stepped into the batter's box. It embarrassed the hell out of him, especially after the guys on his team started calling him "Little Buzzsaw." Luckily, he had a talent for making line drives into centerfield that got him on base almost every time he went up to bat, so the nickname eventually became less a sign of derision and more a show of respect.

But now that he was older, did he really blame his father for being an irresponsible monkeyman who preferred spending his time with aphids and squirrels rather than taking a ground-level interest in his very own wonderful son?

Yes, he had to admit that he did. To tell the truth, it pissed him off immensely.

"You wouldn't know it to look at me," Captain Nitt-Witt said, "but I was young once. I had a woman who loved me. She wanted to start a little family. I was flush back then—this is, oh, about 1928 we're talkin' about here…. I'd just paddled a cigar box canoe across San Francisco Bay. Lots of people said it couldn't be done; I'd laid bets that it could. When the time came around to collect, I had a big enough stake to buy the land where I ended up building Nitt-Witt Ridge. But I wasn't set on calling it that at first. Mathilde was my wife by then and she wanted to name it Mount Avalon, or some dang romantic thing. I forget….

"Anyhow, I got her pregnant, there were complications, she died giving birth. End of story. Except that it drove me a little nuts. Flat-out crazy, is more like it. I started building—to keep my mind occupied, y'know?—and I just couldn't stop. Couldn't stop for more'n fifty years… the whole rest of my life. You've seen the results. Along the way, I learned all kinds of magical, mysterious things about life, but the most magical thing of all—sharing my life with another person—I never let happen to me again. Not in the same way as with Mathilde, at least. Sometimes I regret that. In fact, I regret it almost every day… but I had my freedom.

"I guess my point in all this is that your father is a good man— he knows how to love—only right now he needs to find some kind of balance between the love he has for his family and the magical freedom he feels up in those trees. That's something that may or may not happen for him right away. In the meantime, well… I'm sort of in the market for a sorcerer's apprentice."

Philo didn't know what to say. He was having a hard time taking in all that Captain Nitt-Witt had told him. "What do you mean, a sorcerer's apprentice?" he asked.

"Someone to help me out up at the Ridge. Chores like chopping wood, carrying water. I thought you might be just the right guy to do it. You'd live there full-time—get free bed and board and an hourly wage in return. It's just for the summer. When fall comes around, you'll be headed back to school. But for the next three months, the job's yours if you want it." Captain Nitt-Witt paused to give Philo a serious looking over. "Of course, you'll have to ask your folks for permission first."

The idea excited Philo. "I'll ask 'em. *Wow!* That'd be great!" He thought of how jealous his friends would be, stuck with washing cars or busting their butts on crummy newspaper routes while he was spending a whole summer up at Nitt-Witt Ridge.

Captain Nitt-Witt grinned. "Most people don't believe in me anymore, but I think Harley and Calliope will understand."

Philo found his mother in the kitchen making vegetarian burritos with reckless abandon. He sincerely tried to have a rational conversation with her, but Calliope fought him every step of the way.

"I thought he was dead!" she said, smashing open a waxy green bell pepper with the butt of her hand.

"He said he was just resting, " Philo explained.

"Well, if he's not dead, he must be about a jillion years old by now. He could keel over any minute!"

"Look, Mom, it's right on the other side of the forest. It'll be like summer camp, only closer by."

"What's he going to feed you?" Calliope asked, dicing tomatoes and onions with the confidence of the deranged.

"I don't know… worms?"

Philo smirked and let loose a gentle burp that he'd been saving. Calliope, on the verge of tears, laughed instead and hugged him.

"Philo, I love you, damnit. It's not easy letting you go."

"I know. I love you, too, mom."

Calliope wiped away her tears on her tie-dyed apron and collected herself. "Besides," she said, "now that your father won't get his butt down out of the trees, you're the only person I have to talk to."

Philo patted her arm. "You've got lots of friends, Mom."

"I know, but they're all hippies."

"So are you."

"If it wasn't for your father, I could have been an Certified Public Accountant by now."

"There's still time."

Calliope kissed Philo on the cheek. "Shut up, please. I'm trying to feel sorry for myself."

Philo leaned his motorcycle against the trunk of Brautigan's Oak. Harley was already sitting on one of the tree's limbs, waiting for him with a big burlap sack in his lap.

"I brought you some magic beans." Harley dropped the sack at Philo's feet.

"This for the chickens?"

"Yeah, '*cluck.*' Resinated hemp seeds. Should mellow those mothercluckers out. Turn em' back into vegetari—"

Harley shuddered as he spastically erupted with a screeching "*COCK-A-DOODLE-DO!*" He put his hand over his mouth, as if his sudden crow had been an embarrassing hiccup.

Philo regarded him coolly. Harley took a sudden interest in the backside of a leaf.

"Dad, Captain Nitt-Witt asked me to help him out up at the Ridge. He wants me to move up there for the summer."

"I know. Your mom told me... 'cluck.' We both think you should go for it."

"Really?"

"Yeah." Harley was still interested in that leaf. "He's a smart old guy... you'll learn a lot from him."

"This is so cool!"

Philo wasn't doing a very good job of hiding his excitement. He wished he'd been more subdued when his father turned to look at him with wistful, red-rimmed eyes that suddenly seemed much older than they'd ever seemed before.

"Captain Nitt-Witt was like a hero to me when I was growing up," Harley said, his voice coming from someplace far away. "But I've only met him a few times, 'cluck.' And I never got invited up to the Ridge. You're lucky, Philo."

"I know. I'm going up there today. I mean, if that's okay...."

"Sure, but take care of those chickens first."

"You bet!"

Philo started up his Vincent Black Shadow.

"Hey, uh, Philo?" Harley had to shout to be heard above the motorcycle's roar.

Philo shut the engine down. "Yeah, Dad...?"

"Sometimes... well... I know you might think that—'cluck'—that I'm just not—"

"Dad?"

"Um, what?"

"I'm really glad you're my father. You make everyone else's dad seem boring."

"I'm glad you think that, Philo... 'cluck.' Because, you know, I worry about that sometimes."

"About what?"

"About whether I've been a good dad."

"To be honest, I just wish you were around more."

"Yeah, well—"

Philo started up his motorcycle again. "Gotta go. But I love you. I'll see you later. And thanks for the seeds!" Philo set the burlap sack on his lap, waved a V-fingered peace sign at Harley, and then sped off across the warm, sunny field.

Harley watched him go. Then he went back to his leaf contemplating. He was hardly at peace.

8

HANDSOME HANK, HIS HENPECKING

andsome Hank was happy with his fat sack of mail on his back—never mind his hangover. He was a balding bear of a man with a yellow beard and bad teeth—a loyal and devoted emissary of the United States Postal Service. Neither wind, nor rain, nor a shitstorm of tequila could keep him from his rounds.

Before he'd found his true calling as a mailman, Handsome Hank had been a fencing contractor. He'd put up fences around just about everything: ranchlands, suburban lawns, swimming pools, spas, the odd dog run every now and then. He'd once even built a fence around a pizza parlor patio. That was a fine piece of work, all redwood in funky diagonal slats and four-by-four posts with a little gargoyle heads carved on top of each one. The gargoyles all bore a slight familial resemblance to Handsome Hank's own striking visage. He wasn't named Handsome Hank because he was handsome, after all....

The rich guy who owned the pizza parlor never got around to paying him. Handsome Hank tried all the usual methods of receiving payment for services rendered: invoices, phone calls, certified letters. He was simply ignored. One day Handsome Hank decided he'd had enough—it was time for more extreme measures. First, he fortified himself with whiskey, and then he strolled into the pizza parlor wearing a pair of roughed-out buckskin boots— and nothing else.

Handsome Hank's nudity was awesome to behold. His beergut, vast and hairy, approximated the size of a wine barrel. His buttocks were tiny and sunburned. But most impressive was his elephantine male organ, hanging purple and forlorn in the crevasse beneath the hairy dome of stomach, as if one of Handsome Hank's gargoyles had come to life and was drowsing there upside-down.

The pizza parlor was almost filled to capacity with a lunchtime crowd. Handsome Hank took a seat at the bar. All eyes were upon him as he ordered a pitcher of Budweiser and told the pimpled young man behind the counter that he wasn't leaving until he was paid for the fence he'd put up out in back. The pimpled youngster volunteered to call the pizza parlor's owner. Handsome Hank said that would be fine.

Nora Biddle-Whitney, silver-haired Editor-in-Chief of the *Pine Bluff Insurrectionist,* arrived on the scene before the owner could be found. She shot some nice profiles of Handsome Hank with her antique Leica, at angles suitable for a family newspaper. Then she got out her famous blue spiral notebook and goaded Handsome Hank and those around him into giving her some colorful quotes.

The pizza parlor soon had the atmosphere of a rowdy party. At one point, Handsome Hank got an erection and pounded it against the bar railing as he demanded more pretzels. Lost in her pursuit of journalistic truth, Nora cried out for a tape measure.

The owner of the pizza parlor eventually showed up and wrote out a check to Handsome Hank that paid the bill for the fence in full. Only then did Hank deign to put on a pair of red bikini underpants lent to him in the bathroom by a friendly cowboy. He was applauded upon his return.

Handsome Hank resumed his place at the bar, displaying his new cowboy underpants with a fierce pride as he drank two more pitchers of beer. There was a lot of backslapping. Then he threw up—but at least he was cheerful about it. It looked like the party would never end.

Nora's article came out a week later. It seemed to approve of Handsome Hank's insurgency, in a playful, backhanded sort of way. There was even a coy reference to the size of his penis. Handsome Hank found himself being lauded as the town hero. His notoriety helped spur him on to new heights of drinking and fornication. But he hadn't counted on his reputation for craziness turning out to be bad for him in a strict business sense. Clients worried about him showing up at their sites naked. Over the next few months, his fencing contracts dried up on him.

Which led, of course, to the postal exam and his present happy circumstance as Pine Bluff's most fabulous mailman.

Handsome Hank trudged up the road to Mrs. Andersen's house humming the bass line to "In-A-Gadda-Da-Vida." The sky was overcast, but it was hot and muggy—earthquake weather. The green meadow grass seemed to be writhing in the heat, and he would have sworn the clouds were sweating. His tequila hangover was providing him with a somewhat mystical view of life.

Mrs. Andersen's place was the last house on his route, so he was able to make the long walk out there while his mail sack was at its lightest. It was a good thing, too, because Handsome Hank was so hot that all he wanted to do was take off all his clothes and climb into a cool, mossy horse trough to go to sleep.

He wondered what Mrs. Andersen would do if she found a naked mailman in her horse trough. Would she dial 9-1-1? Try to seduce him? Bring him a glass of iced tea? Probably just more fodder for the *Pine Bluff Insurrectionist,* however it turned out.

When Mrs. Andersen's white picket fence came into view, Handsome Hank noticed something weird. Chickens were lined up along the path. They were also perched on top of the fence posts, like the gargoyles he used to carve. As he approached, the chickens stopped their usual, constant clucking and stared at him ominously.

Handsome Hank wasn't humming "In-A-Gadda-Da-Vida" anymore. He'd started thinking about that Hitchcock movie, *The Birds.* But that was about a bunch of killer seagulls that went around blowing up gas stations and pecking everyone's eyeballs out. Chickens were stupider than gulls, and besides, they couldn't fly worth a shit.

Still, there were a hundred beady eyes staring up at him with dull yellow hatred.... Handsome Hank thought it best to proceed with caution.

Mrs. Andersen's mailbox was at the end of the white picket fence. All he had to do was shove the latest Publisher's Clearinghouse missive into it, and then he could get the hell out of there. It never occurred to him that he might let Mrs. Andersen know a day later that she may have already won over a million dollars.... Neither wind, nor rain, nor a hundred pissed-off chickens would keep him from his rounds.

Handsome Hank shuffled toward the chickens in his steel-toed mailman's boots. *Try pecking through those, you fuckers,* he telepathically communicated to the chickens. They parted ahead of him and fell in behind him to cover his footprints on the dusty path. He was almost to the mailbox. Chickens surrounded him, silent and menacing. He couldn't even see the ground.

As he reached to open the mailbox, a chicken perched on the fence next to it and hissed at him like a viper. Handsome Hank immediately thought of death by chicken venom, illogical as that seemed. He didn't take his eyes off the hissing chicken as he fumbled for the sacred Publisher's Clearinghouse envelope.

Brief as the interval between the flash of a nuclear denotation and the first shock wave, Handsome Hank's vision was obscured by a blur of white feathers, followed by a sudden whirring of wings. A chicken had launched itself out of the mailbox into his face.

"Ghah! Crap!" cried Handsome Hank. He fell to the ground. The chickens descended upon him.

Handsome Hank felt his body wracked by a thousand bloody pecks, as if under assault by a tiny but determined army of sewing machines. His arms and legs were useless against so many vicious chickens. As he sank into the pool of his own nothingness, the vague music of their clucking blossomed in his ears. From somewhere above and beyond that, Handsome Hank thought he heard harsh, metallic laughter.

Then he felt the peck of one giant goddamned rooster.

Philo parked his motorcycle in the shade of Mrs. Andersen's henhouse and set the sack of hemp seeds on the ground. He walked back to the white picket fence where he had seen a dark blue hat in the dust near the mailbox, crushed so flat that it looked like a stain. He picked it up. It was a mailman's hat. Cool. *Finders keepers,* thought Philo as he walked back to the henhouse.

The henhouse was empty. "Mrs. Andersen, where's your crazy chickens?" he asked of the dust motes dancing in shafts of sunlight. Mrs. Andersen wasn't there, either.

Handsome Hank was there, but only partially. His severed hand rested among five perfect white eggs in a hen's nest, not more than a yard away from the feed trough where Philo dumped the hemp seeds.

The hand vibrated ever so slightly as Philo started up his motorcycle and rode away.

9

CAPTAIN NITT-WITT, HIS CRAFTY RAFTING

The afternoon was warm and creaky. The pine trees sounded like they were scratching their armpits and cracking their spines. Philo headed through the forest to Gargoyle Creek, where Captain Nitt-Witt had promised to meet him. He found the Captain on the bridge with his lips puckered up around the nipple of a doughnut-shaped Donald Duck inflatable wading pool.

"Philo! How'd it go?" Captain Nitt-Witt set the wading pool aside, fully inflated. "What'd your folks say?"

"They said okay!"

"Mighty gracious of them."

Philo had to agree. "They're pretty cool, as parents go."

Captain Nitt-Witt grabbed Donald Duck by the throat and hauled him over to the edge of the creek, where an identical wading pool was already bobbing in the water. The Captain sat down in his wading pool and indicated for Philo to do the same, saying, "C'mon, let's see if you float."

Philo climbed into the second wading pool, pinching Donald Duck's beak to steady it. "Where'd you get these dorky things?" he asked.

"These are the magic ships that take men deep into the mystery of their souls." The Captain let loose with a guttural *"Har, har, har!"*—like a jocular pirate.

What a maniac… Philo thought to himself.

"Shove off, matey!" Captain Nitt-Witt shouted.

The wading pools drifted out toward the center of the creek. To Philo's unspoken amazement, they started floating upstream, toward the gargoyle.

A chilly breeze swept through the forest, picking up dead leaves and making them skitter across the rocks like dried-out tarantulas. The shadows behind the gargoyle seemed to darken. Philo thought back to his sixth Halloween, when he would've sworn that the gargoyle was about to reach out and grab him. He had that same premonition now.

He heard a sudden whirr of wing beats, accompanied by a chorus of frantic rodent squeals. He looked up to see a cloud of bats and luminous green lunar moths rising from behind the gargoyle's wings.

"What the heck is going on here?" Philo tried to back-paddle, but the pull of the current was too strong. He yelped when he saw a churning whirlpool appear at the gargoyle's feet.

"Don't be scared, Philo," Captain Nitt-Witt said. "This is just the back door to the Ridge."

Stone turned to flesh and the gargoyle leaned forward with a predatory grin. Its talons were waving like spider legs, clicking with the sound of knives. Philo anticipated his own death, or at least a bad haircut. Then his wading pool shuddered and squeaked and went plunging into the whirlpool. The next thing Philo knew, he was roaring down a watery passageway, having just eluded the gargoyle's grasp.

Whooping, clutching the necks of their respective Donald Duck inflatable wading pools, Philo and Captain Nitt-Witt rode a flood of water down a mossy chute of stone. They splashed down into an underground river fed by at least six major waterfalls and many smaller ones—all gushing from caves high up in the stalactite-dripping limestone cavern surrounding them. The noise of falling water rang out so loud that Philo felt it was part of him. The cool, spray-laden air seemed to be breathing him. He was having trouble distinguishing where his own body left off and the world around him began.

It should have been pitch-dark in there, but it wasn't. The river water seemed to glow, casting weird filigrees of light everywhere.

"Swimming pool lights," Captain Nitt-Witt explained. "I put 'em in myself about twenty, thirty years ago. It was a lucky thing, me finding this underground cavern. Saved the necks of a whole bunch of my Japanese buddies back around World War II. We used to come down here and shoot the breeze, chase the dragon, play a little poker… anything to pass the time. They said they liked it better than being cooped up in a damn internment camp somewhere."

"So you really did that?" Philo asked as the noise of the waterfalls was left behind them.

"Did what? Hid a few of my friends from a bunch of policy dupes following a wrongheaded government order? You bet I did. And I know you'd do the same."

Philo took pleasure in thinking that he would, too.

The river soon dwindled to a placid black stream that carried them into a small cave. The cave was dark, but up ahead its walls were glowing with eerie beams of light. Crawling all about those walls were dozens of slimy leprechauns wearing miners' hats. As Philo's wading pool slowly spun on the current, he saw that he was surrounded. Leprechauns clung to every ledge and crevasse. Some even hung upside-down from the ceiling like bats. He wondered if they were dangerous. They certainly smelled bad.

"Welcome to the Tunnel of Wisdom, Philo," Captain Nitt-Witt said. "You can ask any question you want, and it'll be answered here."

"You mean, like, what's the capital of Idaho?"

The leprechauns erupted in competitive shouting, all of them trying to answer Philo's question at once:

"Stockton!"

"Camarillo!"

"Gristlephlegm!"

"Boise!"

"Indiana!"

"Madrid!"

The shouts degenerated into cries of pain and anger as the leprechauns started beating on each other, hitting and kicking and yanking on beards. The Captain hawked a wad of tobacco spit into the stream. "The trick is," he said, "you have to figure out which answer's the right one."

"That kind of sucks," said Philo.

"That's life," said Captain Nitt-Witt.

"Yeah, that's life all right…" Philo addressed the leprechauns. "Hey! Why are we born only to suffer and die?"

Again, the leprechauns erupted in competitive shouting:

"Misery loves company!"

"Life is a series of soul lessons!"

"Adam ate a bad biscuit!"

"Suffering and death are illusions!"

"Karma is a harsh mistress!"

"Your grandfather was a dogcatcher!"

Fighting broke out again and the answers were lost in wails of leprechaun fury.

"These guys are jerks," Philo declared.

"You have to listen hard to tune in the wisdom from all the static of modern living," Captain told him.

"—or to find the truth hidden in all the bullshit," said Philo.

He'd finally recognized the smell inside the cave.

10

PHILO, HIS FLAMING POOH-BEAR

The stream carried Philo and Captain Nitt-Witt beyond the tunnel full of leprechauns and dumped them into a pool at the lower end of a dark, sooty room with walls of abalone shells over thirty feet high. Philo guessed it to be the basement under Nitt-Witt Ridge, only the Captain wasn't calling it that, exactly.

"You've done well, Philo," the Captain said, tip-toeing through muck and mud to get his wading pool to higher ground. "You made it through the Rapids of Ego-Loss. You kept your head in the Tunnel of Wisdom. Now you get to spend some time in the Furnace of Enlightenment. It heats the whole Ridge."

Philo looked around. The floor of the room was covered with broken toys and old books and water-stained board games. There was a red plastic record player, a bicycle speedometer, a glow-in-the-dark yo-yo, and a dirty stuffed skunk, among other things. It all seemed very familiar.

Then Philo glimpsed a mildewed Winnie-the-Pooh bear with stuffing bulging from its seams and suddenly he knew:

"Hey, this is all my stuff!"

Captain Nitt-Witt nodded. "That's right. All the crap from your past." He picked up a moldering pair of Spiderman pajama bottoms. "I can't believe you even wore these...."

"Dude, Spiderman's cool," said Philo. "Where'd you get all this?"

"Everybody has a cluttered-up room like this, only they usually keep it locked away inside their heads. If you don't clean it up occasionally, it weighs you down, locks you in chains. It gets to be like an overgrown forest that won't let enough light down inside it to let new things grow. Just like in nature, you need a good fire to sweep through every once in a while so life can begin again."

Philo stooped and picked up the fuzzy yellow Pooh-bear. The coal-black eyes still had a friendly, familiar gaze. The simple red bib remained intact, its gold stitching spelling out the name that Philo now whispered to himself—an incantation of all the secret joys and convoluted sorrows of his childhood: *"Winnie…"*

There was a rusty iron furnace shaped like a dragon's head over in the corner—a blacksmith's whimsy, all curling fangs and bulging eyes. Captain Nitt-Witt shuffled over to it and cranked a squeaky wheel. The dragon's mouth opened, revealing a fiery interior. "C'mon…" the Captain said, "it's time you torched Winnie's fuzzy-wuzzy butt."

Philo clutched Winnie to his chest and shouted, "No way!"

"Let the past bear witness against you, Philo—then burn it up. Get yourself free. Like my Japanese buddies used to say, 'There's no enlightenment for those who cling.'" Captain Nitt-Witt stirred the glowing coals in the dragon's mouth, using a baseball bat stamped with an official Willie Mays autograph.

Philo's bat. There were things in that room he hadn't seen or thought about in years.

"Wow, my Official Buffalo Bill Rodeo Jacket!"

"Fascinating…." The Captain turned his back on Philo's tiny, leather-fringed revelation and trudged up a steep abalone shell staircase. He took an old jailor's key from a pocket in his robe and used it to unlock a door at the top of the stairs. The door was made of oak planks held together with a baroque spiderwebbing of ironwork, no doubt fashioned by the same blacksmith who'd made the dragon furnace. It was so heavy the hinges groaned as the door swung open.

"I'll be back when you're ready," Captain Nitt-Witt called down to Philo. "Get to work."

The heavy oak door slammed shut. Philo heard the rattling of the jailor's key in the lock, and he knew he was going to be left alone with his childhood for however long it would take him to get over it.

Time permeated all things in the Furnace of Enlightenment and made them its captives. It was time that silvered in the slowly drying trails of snail mucus on the abalone shell walls. Time quivered in the fake rubber dog vomit that Philo found buried under a time-rotted stack of *Mad* magazines and *Green Lantern* comic books. The pillbugs crawling out of Philo's first baseball mitt carried time on their armored backs. Time would not be denied. It was everywhere, even in the conversational snatches, the hot summer flashes, of Philo's earliest memories.

Frankly, he was getting a little bored.

He'd been sitting there examining the refuse of his youth for several hours or days—he wasn't sure which. The only thing he really knew for sure was that he was getting hungry. He felt dizzy. His guts were churning. Winnie-the-Pooh's dull smarmy gaze was annoying the crap out of him. Philo knew what had to be done.

"Well, Winnie, it's been nice knowing you, but I could really go for a cheeseburger right about now." He stood up in front of the dragon's mouth and tossed his cherished childhood friend into the flames.

Winnie-the-Pooh accepted his fiery fate with a Gandhi-like resignation. His yellow fur blackened. His little red bib exploded in a bright burst of flame. Then something unexpected happened. Sparks spattered and crackled from under the bear's fuzzy rump and he stood up—paws on his hips—and launched out of the furnace like a meteor.

The flaming Pooh-bear flew around the room with weird blue and gold sparks shooting out of his butt. He swooped up around the ceiling, did a loop-de-loop near the furnace flue, and then went hurtling toward the far abalone shell wall. Just as he was about to crash, the wall dissolved. Philo's jaw went slack as he watched Winnie-the-Pooh fly deep into a dark dreamy place where the wall had been just a spilt-second before. Soon he could see only the flames and sparks coming off the tiny, receding bear. Then those flames and sparks coalesced into a single point of light.

Philo found himself watching a scene from his childhood projected onto the space where the wall should have been. It was a home movie, shot and scripted directly from his memory.

He saw himself when he was four, or thereabouts…. It was night. His parents were asleep in their bedroom—Harley curled up, naked, on the platform of dirt and pine needles that he slept on until he made his final transition to the trees, his mother snoring nearby in the four-poster twin bed with flannel sheets. Philo was wearing soaking wet Spiderman pajamas and clutching a very soggy Winnie-the-Pooh to his chest. His four-year-old face was registering shame and guilt and a peculiar sort of anguish. He tugged on the sleeve of his mother's nightdress to wake her up.

"Mom, I wet the bed."

Calliope moaned and rubbed the sleep from her eyes. She did a double take when she saw Philo's drenched pajamas and sopping wet hair.

"Oh, Philo…. Honey, are you sure the volunteer fire department didn't' do this to you?"

The hellish Pooh-bear suddenly barreled trough the scene like an avenging angel, dissolving everything in his wake. As Philo watched, the bear banked to the left and whooshed past his head. The abalone shell wall returned to normal. Still trailing sparks, nearly burnt to a crisp, Winnie made one more pass around the room, then plunged back into the dragon's mouth, where he vanished with a sound like hot oil and firecrackers.

"Wow…" Philo said. The pyromaniac in him was highly gratified.

Cautiously, he put the leather-fringed Buffalo Bill Rodeo Jacket into the furnace and then jumped out of the way. Sure enough, the jacket rocketed out of the dragon's mouth in flames and flew about the room. It went on a crash course for the far wall, and at the last instant the wall dissolved to project another scene from Philo's past.

He saw people sitting around the long wooden picnic table in their dining room for Thanksgiving dinner. His Grandma Charlene was there, along with his Uncle Balmeister and Aunt Virginia, and about nine of his parents' hippie friends. They were all stuffing their faces with his mother's vegetarian food. Philo was there, too, wearing his Official Buffalo Bill Rodeo Jacket, looking proud. He was at least six, maybe seven. He had a plate full of mashed potatoes and string beans in front of him. Suddenly, his little body was wracked by an incredible sneeze. Two disgusting tendrils of snot appeared on his upper lip. All conversation ceased as Philo looked about, dumbfounded by the intensity of the sneeze.

"Philo, wipe your nose, sweetie," his mother told him.

Philo wiped his nose on the sleeve of his rodeo jacket. It left a huge, glistening smear. Several hippies moaned and said, *"Oh, man...."*

"Way to go, pardner," his father said, frowning. *"When the other cowpokes at school ask you what happened, you just tell 'em a horse blew his nose on you, okay?"*

And then it happened. Charlene leaned over and slapped him. Hard. *"Where's your manners, young man?"* she snarled. *"Get up from this table and go clean yourself off."*

Philo started crying.

"Mom. That was out of line," Harley said.

"Someone's got to discipline that little twerp. At the rate he's been going, he may end up even more useless than you are."

Calliope was hugging Philo, asking him if he was all right. He couldn't stop crying.

"How Calliope and I choose to raise Philo is our business," Harley said to Charlene.

She said, *"Well, if you ask me, you're doing it all wrong."*

"Nobody's asking you," Calliope said. *"Look, why can't you just leave us alone?"* Philo was sobbing into her breast.

"Because I'm a mother!" Charlene shouted.

"Well, I'm a mother, too," Calliope said.

"But I'm the older mother."

"Oh, so I guess that makes you the Mother Superior."

Calliope stood up, cradling Philo against her hip. With her free hand, she grabbed a big, squishy clump of candied yams and hurled it at Charlene, shouting, *"Why don't you just get the hell out of here, you witch!"*

The yams spattered against Charlene's dress. She turned and fled out the front door in a rage. Calliope started to cry a little, then Harley smiled at her—and she laughed.

While Calliope—and then Harley—were laughing, on the verge of starting a good-natured food fight, the flaming Buffalo Bill Rodeo jacket flew back through the scene, dissolving everything. The wall went back to normal. There was another crackling explosion as the jacket flapped into the mouth of the dragon furnace and disappeared.

There was no stopping after that. Philo tossed everything he could find into the furnace: tennis rackets, a bathtub submarine, his collection of Wacky Package bubble gum stickers, a ceramic basset hound he sculpted and fired in the fifth grade, roller skates, Pinewood Derby trophies, wind-up chattering false teeth, an 8x10 glossy of a Playboy Playmate of the Year signed "To Philo, Love your sexy eyes. Hugs and Kisses, Trish" that he got when his dad took him to a car show in San Luis Obispo when he was twelve. They all shot out of the furnace to fly, flaming, through the air. The room soon appeared to be swarming with comets.

Philo stood entranced as the firestorm of memories whirled around him. All three walls dissolved to project scenes from his past. He watched three projected versions of his ever-changing self do a puppet dance to discarded emotions. All the secret torments of his youth were played out in front of him. Broken windows, lost toys, stolen candy, lies to his father, foul oaths uttered in the presence of grandmothers—all of his horrible boyhood misdeeds went up in smoke and flames, along with the pain and guilt that had accompanied them.

As each flaming thing returned to the dragon's mouth, the furnace glowed redder with heat. Philo was almost certain he could touch it without getting burned. He was feeling that free.

11

CAPTAIN NITT-WITT, HIS CONTEMPT FOR SOCIAL SECURITY

When the Furnace of Enlightenment was finally empty, Philo sat down wondering what to do next. A few memories still lingered: mental images of his Grandma Charlene, how she'd forced him to eat green tapioca pudding and fried liver, which he hated, while she sat at the table smoking cigarettes; recollections of his mother berating him for leaving soap stains on her sparkling tile surfaces; a dream-like fear of being smothered by Hostess Twinkies....

What was he supposed to do next?

A rhinestone tiara sat in Philo's lap. He hadn't thrown it into the furnace because he was sure it didn't belong to him. Had he ever dressed up as a princess or been crowned Queen of the Helldorado Parade? No, he had not. The tiara was somehow familiar—it made him feel happy and sad all at once—but he was certain it wasn't his.

However, nothing much was happening, so maybe the tiara was holding up the show. With a sigh, he got up and tossed it into the dragon's jaws.

There was a spattering sound and then the tiara rocketed back out of the furnace showering sparks of diamonds and gold. It flew past all three abalone shell walls in a blaze of dazzling fire and all three walls dissolved. They each projected the same scene from Philo's memory. Seeing it, he realized he should have thought of it before.

It was the night of his Halloween flight with Loplop. Mickelodia was down in a dark green meadow doing a twirling dance. She was dressed up as a fairy princess. The rhinestone tiara sparkled in her hair. She tilted her head back to look up at the stars and she saw Philo and Loplop soaring down out of the sky, seemingly from the surface of the moon. Philo waggled his arms and legs like a happy young frog and shouted:

"Mickelodia! Look! I can fly!"

Mickelodia twirled in ecstasy. *"Philo, you can! You really can fly!"*

"Yeah!"

Loplop swooped down and grabbed Philo's hand, leading him away toward Nitt-Witt Ridge.

As Mickelodia watched them go, she shouted: *"Philo, I love you!"*

"What?" he called out from across the distance.

"I love you!"

The fiery tiara boomeranged back through the scene, dissolving everything. It spark-sputtered up near the ceiling and then plunged into the furnace, where it exploded with enough force to shake the dragon's teeth. The dragon's jaws clamped shut and a weird, whooshing noise traveled up through the furnace flue. Philo heard a rattling in the keyhole of the door at the top of the stairs. He looked up and saw Captain Nitt-Witt standing in the doorway with his hands on his bony hips.

"Took you long enough, " the Captain said. "What'd you do, play Monopoly with the bats?"

"What happened to Mickelodia?" Philo asked. "She just disappeared when we were kids."

Captain Nitt-Witt started hobbling down the steep abalone shell staircase. "That's a regular fairy tale, almost," he said. "Her wicked stepmother stole her away and made her a scullery maid in Los Angeles. But don't worry, you'll see Mickelodia again."

"When?" Soon, he hoped.

The Captain reached the bottom of the stairs and put an arm around Philo's shoulders. "When you're ready," he answered. He clapped Philo on the back. "Now climb on up into this old boar's nest. From here on out, you'll be calling it home."

□ □ □ □ □ □ □ □ □

The Captain unlocked the oak door at the top of the stairs and led Philo down a dark hallway wallpapered with posters of airbrushed women in bathing suits posing in front of big airplanes from World War II. Captain Nitt-Witt called it "The Hallway of the Bomber Babes."

Philo guessed it must have made a big first impression on the Japanese guys that hid out with the Captain during the war.

At the end of the hallway a blue door opened onto a room that Philo almost mistook for an underwater grotto. The hardwood floor was painted a shimmering shade of turquoise. Antique glass telephone insulators were stacked in cement up an entire wall and lit from behind, making the whole room glowed liked the interior of an aquarium. The other abalone-encrusted walls had weird stuffed fish jutting from them like the nightmares of moray eels. The fish were fanged and furred. They sported customized accessories like frog legs, tiny bicycle wheels, working turn signals, and hot pink kazoos. A stuffed fish mobile of a similar nature hung over the bed. It made Philo think about what happened when taxidermists went insane.

"This'll be your room," the Captain said.

"Far out…" said Philo.

The next stop on Captain Nitt-Witt's home and garden tour was the tiled courtyard outside. It seemed to be late afternoon. Philo and the Captain walked past oxidized-green copper fountains of mermaids and art nouveau style sea monsters. The flowering trees overhead buzzed with diligent bees. Butterflies flitted among the orchids. Pale Chinese lanterns swayed in the breeze. Two fawns cavorted just beyond the rose bushes.

Philo had seen all that stuff before.

They went back inside. They passed a skinny old Chinese man meditating beneath a fig tree growing in the living room.

"Who's that?" Philo asked.

"That fella? Pay no attention to him," the Captain said. "He's just visiting. I haven't heard a peep out of him since he got here."

"Does he eat?"

"I toss him a banana every now and then."

The Captain directed Philo's attention over toward a huge fireplace made of polished river stones, a ship's anchor, and a few well-placed boulders. "See that? I built it myself. Just about everything in this place I scrounged from the sea."

"You must've had to buy cement, at least. What'd you do for money?"

"Money?" The Captain erupted. "Money is the carrot that leads the jackass! You need enough of it to get by—but only a fool worries about money."

Philo wasn't intimidated. "Well, how'd you get it?"

"You really wanna know?"

An earthquake suddenly blurred the entire living room with motion. Philo heard things squeaking and rattling and breaking. Captain Nitt-Witt staggered over to him and grabbed his shoulders. They were both so off-balance that they leaned into each other and touched noses.

"Quick!" the Captain shouted. "Get under a table!"

Philo scrambled under a burlwood table as the earthquake escalated in its fury. Captain Nitt-Witt opened an umbrella above his head and rocked his elbows to and fro as he commenced an odd little tap dance.

The skinny Chinese man sat in calm meditation under the wildly swaying fig tree. He was bouncing about an inch off the floor.

There was a loud clattering inside the fireplace. Philo turned just in time to see a pregnant grandmother crash out of the fireplace feet first in a cloud of ashes and soot. Her momentum rolled her out onto the carpet, where she laid with crabbed hands tugging at the hem of her long blue skirt. She moaned like a pornographic librarian. Philo knew she was about to go into labor, right then and there. He thought about getting some hot towels, or maybe calling a doctor.

"Look away, boy," she said, unfurling her petticoats, "you don't want to see an old lady's cootchie."

Meanwhile, the air around Captain Nitt-Witt was roiling with psychedelic fog. The Captain stuck his hand out from under the umbrella, checking for rain among the cloudy strands of pink, orange, and purple. As if in answer, a rain of wooden Indian heads fell out of the ceiling, scudding off the umbrella and clunking onto the carpeted floor.

Then the psychedelic fog around the Captain evaporated and the earthquake came to a halt.

Philo crawled out from under the table asking, quite earnestly, "What the hell was that?"

Captain Nitt-Witt grinned and picked up one of the Indian heads, saying, "I suppose I could just apply for social security… but I'd rather engineer these little breaks with so-called 'reality' instead." He tossed the Indian head to Philo. It was beautifully carved from rare hardwood, as solid and heavy as a bowling ball. "These babies go for five hundred bucks a pop down at the Pine Bluff Trading Post. *Captain Nitt-Witt's Indian Head Specials!*" The Captain had allowed an undignified crow to sneak into his voice, reminding Philo of his father.

"Can I have one to keep in my room?" Philo asked.

"Sure! It's no sweat off my nuts."

"Thanks." Philo picked up the carved bust of a beautiful Indian princess—Pocahontas as a sultry movie starlet. She would be nice to look at, he thought, before he went to sleep… although she might make him more prone to horny dreams.

Over by the fireplace, the pregnant grandmother groaned. Slick, wet little mongrel puppies were crawling out from under the tent of her skirt. There were half a dozen of them, and apparently a few more on the way.

Philo asked the obvious question. "Is that old lady having puppies?"

"That's one of the hitches with what I do," Captain Nitt-Witt explained. "A few unexpected anomalies always get sucked over my way. But it always seems to have a way of working out for the best."

The grandmother's labors ceased. Eight blinking puppies stood up on wobbly legs, sniffing the air and wagging their tiny tails for the very first time. The grandmother sighed, still flat on her back, and asked, "Lord, oh Lord, what have I done?"

All eight puppies scampered over toward the sound of her voice. They started licking her wrinkly cheeks, tumbling in her gray grandmother's hair—an assault squad of hot puppy breath and squirming puppy love. The grandmother sighed and clapped her hands together, transported to new heights of grandmotherly bliss. "Oh, stop... *stop!*" she laughed. "You're all too cute! I'll never... no, I'll never be lonely again!"

12

CHARLENE, HER MEAN REVERIES

Philo's embittered grandmother, Charlene, sat in her leather wing chair wearing a long-practiced look of distaste. She was not the sort of woman who would ever give birth to puppies, no matter how lonely her life.

She was reading a Harlequin Romance. Television no longer appealed to her. She read two of the books a day, snorting at the smutty parts. They helped keep her mind off her problems, which were legion.

Her son was an effeminate tree climber. His gender confusion was so severe that it had led to a drug problem—she was sure of it. She suspected him of shooting heroin into his neck veins. Even worse, despite her vehement objections he had married an impoverished hippie harlot, a certain Miss Potty-Mouth who was constantly showing off her braless bosom. Together, they had spawned a son, a boy who often ran amok for no comprehensible reason.

If she could just ignore Harley's drug addiction, ignore his hussy of a wife and the asinine antics of his delinquent son, she would no doubt be much better off. But she was Harley's mother and she couldn't help but be concerned.

Charlene was also quite concerned by what nature had done to her over the years. She had once been quite beautiful—regal, even, if the truth were told. The Lions Club had chosen her as their representative in the Helldorado Parade when she was nineteen years old and she'd won, been crowned Helldorado Queen, even though she was married to Roy at the time and that should have disqualified her. But now she could hardly recognize herself as that young girl. Her bottom was at least a yard wide. The folds of flesh hanging from her jowls were like turkey wattles. Her bosom, still ample, was wrinkled and flabby beyond belief. She had liver spots everywhere. Sometimes she thought the spots might even be on her bones.

As if the grotesqueries of aging weren't enough, she was also subject to a peculiar fungus or rash, which at first had been diagnosed as ringworm, but had turned out to be something far worse. It itched like the dickens. She kept her thighs and shins wrapped with duct tape, so she wouldn't scratch. Her doctor prescribed prednisone for her, which she took at three times a day at twice the recommended dosage. It made the itching not quite so unbearable. It also made her stronger and gave her an appetite like a horse.

Charlene bit into a Hostess Twinkie with a savagery that belied her age and infirmities.

As the creamy white filling oozed across her tongue, she recalled her dreams from the previous night: *Dark, hairy things under the bed; a moment of levitation; some man's wiener tickling her earlobe....* Maybe it was Harold Jenkins, editor of the *Pine Bluff Times.* She used to sneak out the window to see him when Roy fell asleep in front of the radio. Harold, her hot lover. Having his way with her, bending her over the linotype machine, talking dirty to her. He was as cheeky as an Army mule, that Harold. Later, they'd make up tiny news stories about insanity, violent death, unrequited love, and public drunkenness. Harold printed them in the next day's edition:

Negro Somnambulist Sets Fire To Courthouse, Pig, Self Butcher Dead of Heartbreak; Manhood in the Meat Grinder Ossified Child Found in Haystack; Docs Battled Our Sisters of Temperance: In League with the Devil?

It was great fun until Roy found out about the affair and did their tiny news stories one better. He dug a hole in the turnip patch and threw in a few sticks of dynamite. He was a mineworker, like most fellows back then. Knew all there was to know about cinnabar. Roy touched off the fuse while Charlene watched from a distance. He waved his hat at her and laid down with his head over the hole, exclaiming, "Here I go and the Lord go with me." Then there was a huge explosion of brains and turnip greens.

Charlene found Christianity after that one.

So much tragedy in her life... Charlene wondered how she'd had the gumption to survive. Her brother Balmeister was an alcoholic. They'd been constantly fighting since the time they were children. He had no backbone, and she was the only one in the family with enough honesty to tell him. Bal was worthless and weak—there'd never been a doubt in her mind. So what if he'd made millions in real estate?

Then there was The Scandal. After Harley was grown and had a boy of his own, she took up with Ned O'Malley, a married man. One day, Ned's wife, Pamela, discovered them engaged in a brisk bout of coitus on the kitchen floor. Pam couldn't admit it was her own fault Ned had strayed. Sex just wasn't fresh with her, Ned said. He cursed the mercurial nature of matrimonial affection, cursed his own naked, unbounded, goat-like lust.

Pam said she intended to buy a gun.

"She just can't understand my deeper needs," Ned lamented.

Charlene understood. Then in her late-forties, she was still a passionate woman. Nothing in the Bible could replace the gratification of the sexual embrace. It couldn't possibly be a sin, provided she didn't have an orgasm—which never, *ever* did. But Pam just couldn't be content with that knowledge. She had to go and rest her head on a pillow in the oven, where she went off to that kind of sleep from which a person never wakes.

That was twice Charlene's fooling around had killed someone. She could tell the people of Pine Bluff were looking down their noses at her. Some were even angry. It was getting time to leave.

She and Ned packed up their bags and moved to Los Angeles, taking Ned's eight-year-old daughter, Mickelodia, along with them. They got married there, thinking it would clear them in the eyes of the Lord. Charlene decided to keep the marriage a secret. She never told Harley or Balmeister. Whenever she chose to visit, she always went alone.

Ned lasted about a year. His end was unseemly. A prostitute convinced him to ingest some fabled drug during the climax to a bit of nastiness involving leather, chains, Cool Whip, and two obedient cocker spaniels named Spic and Span. The drug turned out to be the pesticide DDT. The dose was so toxic to Ned's system that he died of a heart attack within the hour. Charlene had him buried at Forest Lawn and that was that. His life insurance policy paid off handsomely.

So she found herself rich at the age of 50. She also found herself a single mother again. Mickelodia fell into her custody. It turned out to be a convenient arrangement. Since the girl wasn't her own flesh and blood, Charlene felt no urge to coddle her. For the past ten years, Mickelodia had done all the cooking and cleaning in exchange for room and board. Any nonsense from her and Charlene took away her library card, sometimes for as long as a week.

That library card was all Mickelodia seemed to care about. At that moment, her bedroom was full of books by Hermann Hesse, D.H. Lawrence, Tom Robbins, and Marcel Proust.

Proust! That book of his was at least three thousand pages long!

"Silly little bitch," Charlene muttered to herself as her fat fingers groped for another Harlequin Romance. "Wait until she discovers boys."

13

MICKELODIA, HER ESCAPE FROM TYRANNY AND DUCT TAPE

A blue plastic Jesus stood on the toilet tank lid in Charlene's bathroom. His gaze was always serene. He jiggled every morning when Mickelodia scrubbed the toilet bowl, but he jiggled with dignity.

On the morning of her eighteenth birthday, Mickelodia took pause from her labors to consider just what the blue plastic Jesus really meant to her. She realized she thought of him as a sort of holy Ty-D-Bol Man, a tiny seeker who had abandoned his traditional dinghy and neat little yachting cap on a quest for deeper understanding, for union with the Absolute. For the blue plastic Jesus, there could be no more squirting around in suburban sewage systems, hailing incredulous housewives and informing them of the manifold virtues of blue toilet water. Now he was on the Pathless Path, preaching the gospel of the Tidy God within.

Such thoughts were not uncommon to Mickelodia. She had cultivated a "Rich Inner Life" to compensate for being stuck in the same house with her stepmother in Los Angeles.

They lived in a bungalow ghetto just off of Melrose. All the houses were the same: pastel stucco boxes with bars on the windows and the semi-obligatory palm trees out in front. Their neighbors were Mexicans and Koreans and old white people. Mickelodia wasn't happy there. It had never felt like home to her.

The home she remembered was in Pine Bluff. If it had been up to her, she never would've left. Unfortunately, her stepmother, Charlene, had barreled into her life ten years ago like a typhoon of bad karma, sweeping away everything and everyone she had ever loved. Mickelodia was only eight at that time, but even then she knew Charlene was somehow responsible for her mother's suicide, and a year later, her father's death. The move to Los Angeles was only another part of the woman's evil schemes.

Charlene was just awful, a tyrant. Mickelodia wanted to run away and hide from her forever—but she didn't know how she would survive. She had no friends; Charlene left her no time for them. The streets were full of predators: junkies, thieves, whores and bums. They left vomit on the sidewalks and used-up condoms in the driveways. Mickelodia wished they would all take the time to read Krishnamurti and get enlightened, but she knew that wasn't going to happen anytime soon.

The people who were successful in Los Angeles were just as predatory in their way. They hid behind sunglasses and car phones, constantly calculating the algebra of other people's needs. Just being in the same room with the sunglasses and car phone crowd made Mickelodia feel like a leprous midget. She felt like she was being excluded from some secret society whose members took endless meetings in hives of skyscraper steel, where a kind of alien lizard-language was spoken that she would never understand.

She needed to believe that somewhere people were different. Somewhere people were *wonderful.* So she dreamed of a place where car phones were outlawed and money didn't matter much. She dreamed of Pine Bluff.

"Screw L.A.!" she said, with a particularly vigorous scrub of her toilet bowl brush.

In the Pine Bluff of Mickelodia's dreams, no one was ever mean or egotistical. Everyone lived in a web of gentle hippie magic, connected by threads of love and serendipity. The mayor wore blue jeans. The Tao was required reading in high school. The streets were shaded by elms, oak trees, and Monterey pines taller than any buildings. When two grown men couldn't link their hands around a tree's trunk, Pine Bluff threw a party and gave the tree a tire swing. The tire swing count was a source of civic pride. Anyone could tell you the number.

A creek ran through the center of town. You could fish for trout from the back porch of Wilfred Logan's General Store—but you had to use flies. Wilfred disapproved of bait.

Water wheels and solar panels provided most of Pine Bluff's energy. Almost everyone practiced a trade—from blacksmithing to zither stringing—so that very few goods were ever brought in from the big cities. Bartering was a way of life; cash rarely changed hands. Mickelodia imagined she could get everything she needed, which was really very little, by growing a simple garden and bartering her natural skills as a babysitter, a reader of bedtime stories, a gatherer of wildflowers….

"Mickelodia, hurry up in there, you detergent-sniffing trollop!" her stepmother bellowed at her from the living room. She sounded like a toad with a megaphone. Mickelodia could picture Charlene in her leather wing chair, duct tape wrapped around her fat cheesy legs, a Twinkie stuffed in her fat flapping mouth, a Harlequin Romance in her fat greasy hand.

"The stove needs cleaning, too!" the Toad Lady screeched.

Mickelodia sighed and finished up her scrubbing. In Pine Bluff, she dreamed, the self-cleaning toilet had already been perfected. Vicious stepmothers were beset upon by opossums….

Upon entering the kitchen, Mickelodia briefly genuflected in front of the white plaster Madonna hanging above the stove. "Hail Mary, full of grease…." She sprayed a fine mist of household cleanser about her, like smoke from a censer, and commenced the ritual wiping of the kitchen counters.

"Don't use up all my Handi-Wipes," the Amphibious Bitch From Hell croaked from the next room.

Later, Charlene's neurotic German shepherd, Tartuffe, surprised Mickelodia as she was vacuuming the Oriental rug in her stepmother's bedroom. The big dog bounded into the room like a puppy, almost knocking her over in his frenzy to attack the vacuum cleaner. With a high-pitched bark, he pounced on the Hoover as she pushed it across the floor. Much growling ensued. Mickelodia decided to let Tartuffe devour his prey. She stood the vacuum cleaner upright and screwed in the hose attachment at the back, so she could go after the dust bunnies under Charlene's bed.

Without so much as a warning bark, Tartuffe pounced again, just as she was switching the vacuum over to the hose attachment. The resulting farting noise told her, without even having to look, that Tartuffe's tongue had been sucked up the extension tube.

"No, Tartuffe. Oh god!" Mickelodia and Tartuffe engaged in an absurd tug-of-war, she pulling gently on the hose, Tartuffe straining with all four paws, eyes wide with doggy horror, as his long pink tongue grew longer by the moment. Mickelodia had a giggling fit, then she yanked the vacuum cleaner cord out of the wall socket and the farting noise came to an end.

Tartuffe was free.

He paced the Oriental rug in quick circles, flicking his tongue in and out of his mouth as if he was reacquainting himself with it. He shuddered and shook his head.

When the next dog sniffed his butt, what a story it would tell!

A shallow groan alerted Mickelodia to her stepmother's presence. Charlene was teetering in the doorway, leaning heavily on her cane. The duct tape around her legs was crinkled and peeling.

"You randy little witch," she said, "how dare you abuse my puppy."

"What do you mean, Charlene?" Mickelodia was still sitting flat on the floor, weak from the giggles.

"Sucking on my poor puppy's tongue. You'll give him nightmares!"

"It was his own fault!"

"I should report you to the SPCA."

"Oh, *right.*"

"You don't think they know how to deal with smart-mouthed little tarts like you? They have ways…."

A happy thought occurred to Mickelodia. She'd finally had enough of her stepmother's perpetual bitching—and she didn't have to take it anymore. She stood up and looked Charlene right in the eye as she said: "Today's my eighteenth birthday. You may be my stepmother, but you don't own me anymore."

Mickelodia knocked the vacuum cleaner over with a toss of her hand and walked right past her astonished stepmother, heading for the front door.

"Where do you think you're strutting off to, Missy?" cried Charlene.

Mickelodia was already out on the front porch. "I'm free. According to the laws of this great land, I don't have to be a slave to gross old cows with duct tape on their knees anymore—" an afterthought—"unless I need the money."

"You need the money!"

"Sorry, but I don't." Mickelodia was feeling at once giddy and totally in control. "I'm going to Pine Bluff."

The front door slammed shut.

"Fine!" Charlene yelled after her. "Go on! Live with a tribe of filthy hippies! I hope the lice eat you alive!"

The ones you love always hurt you the most, Charlene thought bitterly.

She derived great comfort from the sanctimonious lies she told herself.

14

MRS. ANDERSEN, HER DENUDED WOLFHOUND

Mrs. Andersen was shaving the fur off Bart, her Irish wolfhound, with a pair of electric sheep shears. The reason for Bart's de-furring was not lice, but a chance encounter with a skunk. Bart was always tangling with something unsavory. Once, he came home with a bandy-legged trout between his jaws. Trout weren't supposed to have legs, but this one did, just like a frog. Another time, Bart got an eye infection from going after a poisonous Big Sur spitting mole. Almost went blind. So this was nothing—his third utter and complete humiliation by skunk musk.

You'd think he'd learn….

A commercial appeared on the television that Mrs. Andersen had set outside on top of an upended garbage can so she could watch *Wheel of Fortune* while she worked. The commercial was for a feminine hygiene product that Mrs. Andersen was long past using, so she turned to Bart and said: "I know you don't like being naked, big fella, but how else will you ever be fresh and unscented after wrestling a skunk?"

The question was rhetorical. Bart merely shivered and made no response. He had to admit that he stunk.

Smells…. Mrs. Andersen had experienced a lot of them in her lifetime. She thought back on some of the more memorable ones. What came to her first was the smell of Mr. Andersen's farts in bed. How shocked she'd been to hear them when they were first married. He used to just heave them out while he was fast asleep… unholy sputtering groans from his sphincter that stunk to high heaven. They always woke her up. It sounded like the very devil himself was talking under the sheets. She took to keeping a bottle of French perfume next to the bed: "L'Air du Printemps." Used it to mist the air whenever Mr. Andersen let loose another stinker. Now she couldn't even smell French perfume without thinking she smelled a fart, too.

Mr. Andersen had ruined Paris for her. Not that she'd ever gone far from Pine Bluff—but if she had….

Other smells came to mind. Dishwashing soap and bacon grease. Percolating coffee. Freshly mown hay. That smell of ammonia and old straw in the henhouse. Those were some of her favorite smells. They smelled like her life.

Then there was the very odd smells, the once-in-a-lifetime smells. That time an old cougar came down out of the hills and sprayed on her front porch. The smell of the cotton candy machine that caught fire at the Mid-State Fair in 1952 or '53. That crazy Chinese salesman who came out to the farm trying to sell her ginseng roots and little silk purses that smelled of mothballs. The stench of a dried-up sand shark on the beach, a rotten elephant seal, a dead bear in the henhouse, and Ernest, poor Ernest…

Why did death always have such a stink to it? Even Mr. Andersen smelled a little gamey after she found him dead of a heart attack on the kitchen floor a few days before his 71st birthday. She was all alone now… if she died, she might not be found for weeks. And then just imagine the stink!

Those poor undertaker people… why in heaven would anyone choose to go into that line of work?

The sound of distant clucking brought Mrs. Andersen out of her olfactory reveries. "Oh listen, Bart… the chickens are back." She cupped her hands to her mouth and cried out like a nightingale with a toothache: *"Here chickie-chickiee-CHICKIEEES!"*

Mrs. Andersen's chickens proceeded along the dirt path to the farmhouse in a very orderly, unchicken-like fashion. They were marching in military lockstep, row upon endless row of them, each row ten abreast. These were serious chickens. Storm trooper chickens. And in their midst, a larger figure accompanied them on two huge, vaguely reptilian feet.

Mrs. Andersen saw none of this. She was pointing her face up toward the sky, concentrating on her chicken-calling: *"Here chickie-chickie…."*

Bart, however, was aghast.

A cloud passed in front of the sun. Mrs. Andersen paused to adjust her glasses. *"Here chick—"*

A robotdinosaurooster?

"Oh my…" Mrs. Andersen said as a scaly, partially feathered hand lunged for her throat.

She was lifted into the air as if she weighed nothing at all. *"Upsy-daisy!"* she squeaked. Then she started strangling. She felt her oversized golf shoes go flying off her wildly kicking feet.

Her chickens had betrayed her! She had a feeling she wouldn't get to watch the end of her game show. Not unless Bart came to the rescue.

Bart did no such thing.

Bart watched his former owner get deboned by a gigantic Sunbeam electric carving knife. That was something new. He sort of wanted to go over there and take a closer look, but he felt self-conscious about not having any fur. Chewed-up shoes floated through his memory. He wondered who would feed Alpo to him now. There was the scent of something tragic in the air, something nearly as tragic as not having enough Alpo.

The chickens were eating Mrs. Andersen.

Bart wondered how she tasted. Those intestines looked like big greasy sausages.

Once, when he was trotting around with a spitty tennis ball in his mouth, Mrs. Andersen had looked at him and laughed. Her laughter had stirred something deep within him. It had made him mourn for his wild ancestors—his snarling, yipping, biting, howling ancestors. They were unsullied by civilization, too cunning for domestication. They bared their teeth and tasted hot blood and bone. Plumes of steam rose up from the animals they gutted. Their hackles were made hoary with snow. Bart felt this heritage stirring in his own blood, and he vowed that day to go out and bite the mailman.

But the chickens had gotten to the mailman first, darn them.

He looked up at the big creature wielding the carving knife and thought, *Maybe we can be buddies...*

Mickelodia's journey to Pine Bluff was uneventful. All she'd had to do was go into the Mexican grocery store and explain her plight to Mrs. Soto, who'd been selling Charlene's Twinkies to Mickelodia for the last ten years. An agreement was reached in which Mrs. Soto would lend Mickelodia money for bus fare to Pine Bluff—plus two quarts of orange juice, almonds, and some deli-sandwiches—in exchange for her promise to scout the new location for grocery store potential. Mrs. Soto wanted to get out of Los Angeles as badly as Mickelodia did.

It was getting dark when the bus finally dropped Mickelodia off in front of the Pine Bluff General Store. Wilfred Logan—if he still owned the place—had closed up for the night. In fact, all the shops were closed. Mickelodia thought of all the people she had known in Pine Bluff, and who would be most likely take her in on such short notice. She decided on Mrs. Andersen, who had been like a grandmother to her when she was growing up. It didn't matter that Mrs. Andersen's house was a ways out of town. Mickelodia had been sitting for about seven hours. It would be good to stretch her legs.

When she got to Mrs. Andersen's, she didn't find anyone home. She rang the front bell, then went around to the back and knocked on the kitchen door, but no one answered. For all she knew, Mrs. Andersen was dead. Ten years had gone by, after all, and even back then Mrs. Andersen had been old.

Mickelodia decided to spend the night in the forest. As she walked from behind the house into Mrs. Andersen's driveway, she saw a nude wolfhound prancing in the moonlight. He was carrying some small creature, tossing it up in the air with his teeth, then pouncing with his front paws and doing some frisky barking when it hit the ground. As Mickelodia passed, she took a closer look and decided the dog had a dead mouse.

Actually, it was Mrs. Andersen's nose.

15

CALLIOPE, HER WILD-ASSED LONGINGS

alliope was adjusting to being alone. If Harley wanted to spend the rest of his life up in the trees like some giant chipmunk with a hard-on, that was fine, she could deal with it—so long as he didn't neglect his duties as a husband and a father, which she had to admit, he didn't. Sure, it was a little weird standing under the walnut tree out in back and saying, "The phone bill is $46.73 and the gas company wants $27.86—then having the checks drop from the branches like leaves—but hey, she could handle it. She believed that "Till death do you part" crap. Probably dumb on her part, but she was stubborn.

It had gotten harder after Philo went to live with Captain Nitt-Witt. She missed having someone to look after, someone to talk to in the evenings after the day's work was done. For a while, she did all of the things she'd never had time to do while she was raising a family. She cleaned out the cupboards, reorganized her spice rack, made a dozen quarts of green tomato relish, wrote letters to every old friend she could think of, and wallpapered the kitchen ceiling. Then all those things were done and she passed the hours wondering what to do next.

She was lonely. She couldn't help it. She wasn't a big fan of solitude. She thought it sucked. She wasn't cut out for peace and quiet on a long-term basis. She didn't want to take up quilting. She didn't want to curl up with a good book. She was a woman, damnit. She had wild-assed longings.

One night, when Calliope's wild-assed longings were running particularly high, she decided to take action. First, she relaxed in a long, hot, herbal bath. Then she anointed her naked body with sandalwood and patchouli oil. She lit several candles and turned the lights down low. In the flickering candlelight, she pinched her nipples, sending intense psychosexual thoughts out to Harley. She gave Harley ample time to pick up on those thoughts. Then she put on her sexiest hippie dress and went outside to stand under the walnut tree.

Harley failed to show up.

Damn him. Just like a man... Calliope thought.

She sat in the tire swing and spun herself around. Frogs were croaking in the evening calm. Crickets chirped. The stars spoke of more permanent things. Calliope grew wistful. She started talking to her absent husband.

"Harley, can you hear me? This is your wife. Remember her? She's the one who groaned like a grizzly bear singing lullabies while you made love to her. She kissed the sweat off the back of your neck when you bent over to sharpen your chainsaws. She watched you dance the mambo in your electric blue boxer shorts. Where are you? I'm lonely."

There was a rustling of leaves overhead.

"Harley, damnit! Get your butt down out of that tree right now or lose me forever."

Harley descended on blue tree climber's ropes. He looked like a gangly blonde spider. Ratchets clicked as he manipulated the ropes to bring himself horizontal with Calliope's face. His expression was dark and romantic—the tree climber turned Byronic hero.

Calliope rolled her eyes. "Oh, great. Do you get cooties if your feet touch the ground?"

Harley was trying his best to create a mood. He thought of Shelly drowning off the Viareggio coast. "Hi, *'cluck,'*" he said significantly.

Calliope, always a demonstrative woman, spun around and stamped her foot. "*'Hi?'* I haven't seen you for at least a week and the first thing I get out of you is *'Hi!'?*"

"What'd you want me to say? *'Boo?'*"

"How about 'Calliope, light of my soul, love of my life, I'm really, truly goddamned sorry that I haven't visited you—or even taken the time to call or write—because I've been living up in the fucking trees like some idiot spun-out jungle monkey for god only knows how long now.'"

"I love you... *'cluck,'*" It was all Harley could think of to say. He wished he hadn't let that *'cluck'* sneak in there, though.

"Go *cluck* yourself," Calliope replied. "I'm your wife. I deserve better than this."

Oh boy... now she's pissed, Harley thought. He tried to appease her. "What do you want, Clippy?" he asked in a meek voice.

"I want some companionship, damnit!" Calliope was surprised to find herself yelling. She toned it down a little. "And don't call me *Clippy*. I hate that."

Harley had an idea. "Y'know, on my way over here I saw a girl asleep in the forest. Out past Mrs. Andersen's place. Maybe you could take her in."

"You want me to adopt some screwed-up little forest tramp? I want a husband."

"She looked around fifteen or sixteen," Harley continued. "Might make good company."

Calliope's motherly instincts came into play. "Did you ask if she was all right?"

"Are you kidding? People don't believe in kindly woodsmen anymore. If I dropped out of a tree and woke a girl out of a sound sleep, the first thing she's gonna think is *'Rape!'*.... Besides, it's a warm night. She'll be okay."

"Is she a local girl?"

"Actually, she kind of looks like Ned and Pam's daughter, all grown up. *Mickelodia.* Remember her? Long red hair? Sweet angel face?"

"Didn't Philo have a crush on her? She had to leave town with Ned after he and your mother—"

"Yeah, let's not get into that business again."

"Well, I'll go look for her in the morning. But as for taking her in, I don't know… I can't decide right now. I'm still mad at you."

Ratchets clicked. Harley lowered the ropes supporting his feet until he was tilted at a forty-five degree angle to Calliope, almost touching the ground. He had that absurd Byronic look on his face again.

"Mr. Stiffy is very angry with you right now, too," he said.

"Oh he is, is he?" The angry light disappeared from Calliope's eyes. It was replaced by a glint of sexual mischief.

"Very angry. '*cluck*.'"

Calliope reached up under her dress and stepped out of her panties. "Well, we can't have that.…"

With a sigh, Calliope unbuckled Harley's pants and climbed into the web of ropes supporting him. Harley swung himself under her like a human hammock. Ropes strained, ratchets clicked, and the limbs of the old walnut tree creaked as their lovemaking commenced.

A swarm of luminous green moths was attracted by the scent of orchids, blood, and ocean tides that bloomed in the air around them. The twilight sonatas of crickets and frogs seemed to lift Harley and Calliope up on silver wings. Actually, it was the moths, nipping into their skin with a delicacy borne of their nature.

The moths carried the lovers out from under the boughs of the walnut tree in tender flight. Harley and Calliope were too lost in each other to notice the tree and the warm orange glow from the windows of their house being left far below them. They felt safe beneath the celestial dome. They were naked, heaving angels.

The luminous moths carried them still higher, seduced by the pale flame of the moon.

A shudder convulsed the sky that night. The frogs stopped their croaking, and the crickets their chirping, when they heard the stars cry out with a faint but unabashedly ecstatic "*Cock-a-doodle-doo!*"

16

PHILO, HIS TROUT SYMPATHIES

Philo dreamed he was in a pup tent with two pink plastic bunnies—the inflatable kind awarded as carnival prizes. They were almost as big as he was, even though they were only half-inflated. There was something almost cloying about them. The pup tent seemed suffocating.

Philo went over to the mosquito-netted window for air. The bunnies started talking about him behind his back—cute little squeaks from big buckteeth. He couldn't make out what they were saying. He knew the pup tent was pitched in the most magnificent wilderness area imaginable, but he couldn't go outside just yet. It was somehow important for him to stay in the tent and try to figure out why he was with those weird bunnies.

The dream ended when Captain Nitt-Witt opened the door to Philo's bedroom and threw a gunnysack full of live trout on the bed, waking him.

Philo thrashed around like a blind swimmer. A big rainbow trout squirted out of the sack and flapped its tail against his jaw. A modest brook trout nuzzled under his armpit.

"Jesus! Fish!" Philo shouted, slapping them away. Then he saw the Captain standing in the doorway. "You scared the piss out of me," he said.

"Yeah?" The Captain seemed unconcerned. "Well, you wash your own sheets around here. I'm not your mother."

"Where'd you get these?"

"Fifty years ago I stocked the Rapids of Ego-Loss with trout. Rainbows, brookies, and browns. Now whenever I want a meal, eight pound test and a Number Two Dang Samuel Gill Buster hauls those suckers right out of there.

"You're a fly fisherman?"

"One of the best."

"I've always wanted to learn how to fly-cast. D'you think you could teach me?"

"Sure! I wouldn't have an apprentice who didn't know his way around a trout." Captain Nitt-Witt grinned and handed Philo a fish knife. "Today's your first lesson. You're gonna gut and clean these slippery bastards. We're having 'em for breakfast."

Philo looked at the big rainbow on his pillow. It seemed to be gasping, dying from too much air. Its big round eye spoke of resignation to one's fate, confronting one's destiny with a steely resolve. But then—did Philo only imagine it?—the trout shed a tear.

This was a melancholy fish—a thinking, feeling, wondering fish. A fish that wrestled with existential doubt. A fish that could have played Hamlet in a trout tragedy.

"I can't gut this fish," Philo said. "It's still alive."

"Not for long," said the Captain. "Don't ask me why, but life feeds on life on this planet. That's just the way it is. Fish get eaten by men, then men get eaten by fish if the Neptune Society has its way in the end."

"I can't do it. Not while it's staring at me that way." Philo thought it best not to mention that he has seen the trout cry.

"Fish can't do anything *but* stare. They don't have eyelids. Used to though."

Captain Nitt-Witt sat on Philo's bed and picked up the big rainbow to use as an illustration. "It's a shame," he said, "but all the brave and idealistic fish got caught by fisherman a long time ago." He stroked the trout's back as if it were a small dog— perhaps a slimy dachshund. "The day finally came when the only fish left were the timid ones. They all swam around in a constant state of googly-eyed terror, afraid that if they didn't keep their eyes peeled, the next thing they ate might have a hook in it. It got so bad that they wouldn't do so much as blink. Eventually, their eyelids just atrophied away through evolution."

"You're full of shit," said Philo, not unkindly.

"That may be true," the Captain said. "But I'm also hungry. So let's get to work. Here: I'll show you how it's done...."

The oak table in the kitchen had been set with earthenware crockery for two. As Philo looked on, Captain Nitt-Witt dipped halved and headless fillets of trout in cornmeal batter, then set them in an iron skillet crackling with bacon grease.

"Your mother probably took care of this for you," the Captain said, turning the frying trout with his knobby old fingers, "but if you can mix up a batch of psychoactive chemicals, you can cook a trout."

Philo thought about his last visit to his mother, watching her karate chop bell peppers in her own kitchen. "I know it's not cool," Philo said, "but sometimes I miss her."

"Your mother? Wonderful woman. I'd miss her if I was you, too." Captain Nitt-Witt turned the trout again. His fingernails were yellow and thicker than poker chips. "Your mother treated you like a friend. That makes it all the harder to break away from her now, but you've gotta do it."

"Become a man, right?" They'd had this conversation before.

"A manly man."

They both simultaneously hunched over and began beating on their chests like gorillas, going *"whoopf, whoopf, whoopf!"* as loud as they could. Captain Nitt-Witt called it "primal grunting." Very effective for clearing mucus from the bronchial tubes and regulating testosterone flow, or so he claimed. Philo had his doubts.

"Did your mother ever tell you how she got her name?" the Captain asked, standing upright abruptly.

"Nope. It *is* a weird name, though. *Calliope*...."

"Parents can seem so damn mysterious when you're growing up. You think they have all the answers, but hell, they were babies once. They grew up just like you." Captain Nitt-Witt flopped the cooked trout onto plates and sat down at the kitchen table across from Philo. "Did Calliope ever tell you about your Grandmother Wilda?" he asked with an odd stare.

"She's dead?" It was more of a question than a statement.

"Never heard of your Grandma Wilda? Boy, are you in for a story...."

Captain Nitt-Witt proceeded to tell Philo that story as they sat eating their breakfast.

17

WILDA KOLANKIEWICZ, HER HELLDORADO HELLRAISING

Back in 1955, Wilda Palmer was just another Alameda housewife with a drinking problem and a crappy attitude. She had no way of knowing that everything was going to change for her when she walked into a San Francisco art gallery on October 7th.

Her dull but steadfast husband, Mr. Jerome Palmer, had flown out to Denver the previous night for a Hoo-Hoo Club convention, leaving Wilda with a three entire days to herself. Wilda didn't care for Hoo-Hoos—grown men with secret handshakes who drank Scotch in their underpants, then put on blindfolds and bit each other's asses in dark rooms. At least that was the scene as described by Jerome the day after his initiation ceremony. He showed her the teeth marks and the ugly red bruise. Wilda had no compulsion to be shown off in a snazzy yellow dress to a whole convention of such men. And so, despite of her husband's entreaties, she'd remained behind.

On a whim, she'd decided to attend a poetry reading. "Six Poets at the Six Gallery," the flyer on the telephone pole read. Wilda had a vague notion that she might meet a sympathetic poetess there to whom she could air her gripes.

What Wilda walked in on was Allen Ginsberg reading his long, hallucinatory poem of outrage, "Howl," to the public for the first time.

Drunk, arms outstretched in a sharp charcoal suit, Ginsberg wailed out crazy, fabulous sentences that stretched to the end of his breath. Up near the front of the audience, an intense young man with a football player's build and a gallon jug of California Burgundy clutched to his chest started shouting "Go! Go! Go!" in cadence with the lines. Wilda later found out that this young man was Ginsberg's friend, Jack Kerouac.

There must have been a hundred and fifty people in the room that night, some of them soon to be famous. When Ginsberg finished reading, everyone stood cheering, knowing that some barrier had been broken, that something deeply significant had just taken place.

Kenneth Rexroth, the Grand Old Bard of the North Beach poetry scene, stood wiping tears of gladness from his eyes. Gary Snyder, next in line to read, stared straight ahead in blue-jeaned rapture while tapping his own poems against his knee.

Wilda, for her part, really wanted to get laid.

After the reading ended around 11:30, everyone headed off toward Chinese restaurants and Irish bars to discuss what they'd just seen. Wilda got into her car and started driving aimlessly. She couldn't get that first line of Ginsberg's poem out of her head:

"I saw the best minds of my generation destroyed by madness...."

The madness Ginsberg went on to describe seemed preferable to the kind of living death Wilda was experiencing as an Eisenhower-era housewife. She vowed that when Jerome got home she'd divorce him and take back her maiden name: Kolankiewicz. She liked all those hard consonants. It was a name suitable for a Polish witch—just one of the many career options Wilda saw opening up to her, now that she had seen her way to liberation.

She also swore that from that moment on she would only sleep with writers, artists, and angelheaded hipsters. No more dull but steadfast men for her.

She wondered if Allen Ginsberg was queer.

Wilda's determination to sleep with writers, artists, and angelheaded hipsters didn't meet with much resistance. She had the devastating backside and hefty boobs of an adolescent boy's most way-out sex dreams. Plus, straight white teeth and a big whiskey mouth that knew how to pout. She approached the men she seduced as if they were heroic genius-rebels, not the insecure poseurs, drug-muddled egomaniacs, and general

all-around fuck-ups that most of them happened to be. For this generous suspension of disbelief, this willed naïveté, Wilda was rewarded with temper tantrums, faithlessness, bohemian drudgery, and constant touches for money.

Wilda's problem was that after she spent a certain amount of time around a man, he started believe that he really was *a heroic genius-rebel. After this belief took hold, the man began to see Wilda as a pathetic art whore who just wanted to ride on the coattails of his impending fame and fortune.*

How devious of her! How horribly calculating!

But until fame and fortune arrived, Wilda was still good for cooking meals, lending cash, and performing kinky sex acts which the heroic genius-rebel accepted as nothing less than his due. After all, he was expressing himself. He was making a great contribution to humanity— with his incoherent poems, his never-to-be-performed stage plays, his tedious little protest songs, and his smeary, paint-spattered canvases.

Wilda spent almost a year around North Beach, running into this pattern of behavior again and again. Finally, she decided she would stop sleeping with losers and only go after men of genuine talent. She suspected a bona fide genius might be more appreciative of her charms.

Too bad Allen Ginsberg was a fag.

One day a painter friend gave Wilda a smuggled copy of Henry Miller's Tropic of Cancer *and told her about Miller's cult of sex and anarchy down in Big Sur. Wilda was deeply impressed and turned on by the book. She decided to make a pilgrimage to Big Sur to pay her respects to Miller and see if he would lay her.*

Henry Miller turned out to be a disappointment. The Sage of Big Sur had a heavy Brooklyn accent, odd to hear in the midst of all those redwoods. He also had a sweet wife named Eve and two children from a previous marriage, Val and Tony. He didn't come across as the wild, anarchist sex fiend she'd had in mind. Bald, practically, he looked like somebody's grandpa. They talked about poetry, Zen, Jean Varda, and Jimbo's Bop City up in the Fillmore District. He didn't even try to lay her.

But later on, Henry's friend Emil did. Lay her. Boy, oh boy, did he ever!

It was while Wilda was looking for sex and anarchy in Big Sur that she heard about Captain Nitt-Witt and the fantastic castle he was building up on Nitt-Witt Ridge. Wild stories were going around about him: about how he paddled a cigar box canoe across the San Francisco Bay, how he saved Max Ernst from death by curandera *curse down in New Mexico, how he had a cellar full of leprechauns who could answer all the questions to life's mysteries. He sounded like a folk art Renaissance man—just the sort of heroic genius-rebel Wilda had been seeking.*

So she traveled down the coast to Pine Bluff. She lucked out and met Captain Nitt-Witt in Old Camozzi's Saloon, where she had stopped to use the bathroom. They spent all afternoon talking. Other people joined their conversation from time to time. It was Wilda's introduction to Pine Bluff society.

But despite the Captain's guzzling of several quarts of beer—and a snootful of gin rickeys on Wilda's part—he made no attempt to get her in the sack.

What was it, her breath?

"Do you write any poetry of your own?" Captain Nitt-Witt asked her. This, after having listened to Wilda go on and on about Allen Ginsberg's "Howl" for nearly a solid hour.

"No, I…" Wilda ran down the list of excuses in her mind: big city life in general, too much drinking and socializing in particular, babysitting neurotic artist-infants…. None of those excuses seemed worth mentioning.

The Captain had fixed her with an odd stare. "Well, why the hell don't you?"

Why the hell indeed?

Wilda decided she liked Pine Bluff well enough to stay. She rented a little room in town above the Mexican bakery, she got a one-eyed calico cat named Mergatroid to keep her company, she stopped drinking, and she started writing poetry.

Six months later, she had her first book of self-published poems ready for sale. Dead Frogs from Mars, *she was calling it. To help promote it, she was running for Queen of the Helldorado Parade. Captain Nitt-Witt was also a part of Wilda's promotional plans— because he was her best friend and the biggest fan of her poetic efforts… and because he could fly a crop duster.*

Every small town needs a parade to express its individual character, to show what makes it exceptional from all the other small towns everywhere. Sometimes the parade is in tribute to a fruit or vegetable— the Okra parade, the Cantaloupe Parade—that the town produces in unrivaled quantities. Sometimes the parade is in honor of a nationality or religious persuasion—the Swedish Parade, the Seventh Day Adventist Parade—that is shared by the majority of the town's citizens. But sometimes the parade is just an excuse for an entire town to get drunk and collectively wake up in a strange place with vomit on its shoes—like Pine Bluff's annual Helldorado Parade.

When Wilda found out that any unmarried woman living in Pine Bluff could run for the Helldorado Queen, she somehow knew—just knew!—that it was the perfect opportunity to create an audience for her poetry. She immediately went down to the Chamber of Commerce to sign up. She was given a stack of raffle tickets and a form to fill out. Whoever sold the most tickets would win the crown, or so she was told.

At the time, men outnumbered women in Pine Bluff by about three to one. Within days of taking her room above the bakery, Wilda had discovered that the local dating scene was like a game of musical chairs. Almost every single man she ran into wanted her to sit in his lap. Wilda had no desire to date—her poems needed solitude to take root and grow—but she wasn't above flirting, especially when she set up her booth that first day in front of the post office and started selling raffle tickets. Before mid-afternoon, she had to go back to the Chamber of Commerce for more.

With every ticket that Wilda sold, she managed to get in a plug for her book. Dead Frogs From Mars *would be available at all three local bookstores on the day of the Helldorado Parade, if not before. Sometimes, if the man was cute, Wilda put a red lipsticky kiss on the raffle ticket, for a personalized touch.*

When the day of the Helldorado Parade arrived, it was clear to everyone that Wilda had won.

She stood waving on the bow of the Lions Club float, wearing a galvanized bikini and a white satin sash saying "Miss Helldorado Queen 1957." She was the local darling, the coveted one. Cowboys hooted, bicycle horns honked, and the Shriners crashed their go-carts straight into the crowd. Wilda wasn't sure if it was just the parade or her own near-nakedness that was the cause of such rowdiness. Normal guys—bank clerks and plumbers!—were acting like they had whiskey for blood and werewolves in charge of their bones.

As the float was passing in front of Old Camozzi's Saloon, Captain Nitt-Witt flew the crop duster in low over Main Street. He was right on schedule. Wilda waved to him as he roared over the Lions Club float and pulled straight up. He climbed a few hundred feet with the crop duster's tail perpendicular to the ground. Then, just as Wilda had instructed him, he dumped his payload.

Sixty-three gallons of dead frogs fell out of the sky like slimy green hailstones.

In one smooth gesture, Wilda tore off her galvanized bikini top and opened an umbrella above her head, shouting, "Dead Frogs From Mars! Buy the book, then see the movie!"

What most men were seeing were Wilda's fabulous tits.

Then the first frogs landed.

Later, some would compare it to the bombing of Dresden—or the strafing of a small village during the Korean conflict. Frogs assaulted every bouffant in a three-block radius. Frogs filled up the backseat of Mayor Buckley's convertible Packard. A rain of frogs—an endless nightmare horror-storm of deceased amphibians. They exploded in the street like bags of pus wrapped around firecrackers. They left their sickening yellows frog guts hanging from the trees. Bullfrogs as big as cow patties crashed through the roof of Granny Scopalamine's Chicken Pot Pie Tent. Tree frogs tinier than hummingbirds peppered the brim of every cowboy hat in the vicinity.

People started running for cover. The whole town was in a panic, thrown into chaos. Captain Nitt-Witt made another pass in the crop duster, saw what was happening, and in his own words, "felt guilty as hell."

It might have been a disaster if it hadn't been for Damon Finch.

Damon Finch was a Pine Bluff institution. He was a tall man who wore the same brown hat and the same brown tweed jacket every day. He ate burnt toast every morning. Precisely at six o'clock every evening, he walked into Old Camozzi's Saloon and ordered a Tootsie Roll and a glass of port. The glass of port was always filled to the brim.

Even when he was in his eighties, Mr. Finch was able to take the glass over to a bench across the room and sit down without spilling a drop. Once seated, he would discuss the trigonometry of snooker with anyone who cared to listen. Then he would eat his Tootsie Roll and leave. He did this with such regularity that when the ownership of Camozzi's changed hands in 1953, it was written into the contract that Mr. Finch was to be served his glass of port at the same price he always paid for it, and that price was never to be raised.

The price of Mr. Finch's daily Tootsie Roll was left to the vagaries of the marketplace.

It was widely known that Mr. Finch had been a professor of semantics at Harvard for thirty years before he retired to Pine Bluff. For that reason, whenever anyone had a question of a scholarly nature, they visited Mr. Finch in the saloon. Mr. Finch tended to avoid answering the questions in any sort of definitive way, but the questioners always went away well-satisfied, knowing they had taken their problem to the highest intellectual court. The citizens of Pine Bluff had come to rest the weight of their collective dreams on Mr. Finch's narrow shoulders. He was thought of as the living embodiment of dignity and wisdom—Pine Bluff's hero of cool reason.

It is a measure of Mr. Finch's humility that he was unaware of the high-esteem in which his fellows regarded him. He had never married— he had in fact, been out of touch with women since being weaned—and perhaps this lack of contact with the more intuitive sex had made him somewhat obtuse when it came to judging how he appeared to others.

But more likely, he simply didn't want to know.

He lived alone in a two-story Victorian house near the fire station on Burton Drive. The house had been built by a Mr. Franklin E. Drake in 1866. It had no plumbing upstairs and the only heat came from a wood burning stove in the kitchen. Mr. Finch was happy there. He secretly disapproved of electricity, hot water, telephones, and central heating. Such luxuries had never made a man any wiser.

"Great insights of the past are still valid," he once wrote to his pen pal, S.I. Hayakawa. "It is by no means certain that a man who uses a computer and rides in a jet plane can think any better or have more perceptive insights than one who might count on his fingers and ride on a donkey."

Writing was Mr. Finch's great passion. He wrote telegrams, crank letters, essays, manifestos, articles for publication in academic journals, and doggerel verse—all with the single express purpose of establishing a new word in the English language.

The word was Chancequence—*Mr. Finch's term for the fascinating interaction of chance and purpose in human conduct, human thought, and the whole creative process of life on Earth. He recognized Horace Walpole's Serendipity, but thought it too cute, and only concerned with the fortune blending of chance with purpose, whereas his own far superior Chancequence made room for the absurd or even tragic outcome of purpose.*

It was pure chancequence that every year Mr. Finch played the Lions Club calliope to signal the close of the Helldorado Parade. The calliope was in a bright little circus cart that was conveyed along the streets by a team of Shetland ponies. For Mr. Finch's participation in this remarkable exploit, a routine had been worked out.

On the day of the parade, Wilfred Logan would drive the calliope cart to Mr. Finch's door, where Mr. Finch himself would soon appear, clad in his traditional brown hat and brown coat. Mr. Logan would then make a jocular comment to Mr. Finch, something along the lines of "Ready to go?" with a chuckle at the end to signal his complicity in the joke. Mr. Finch would heave out a sigh that implied the effort was a strain on his creaky old bones. Then came the capper to their private comedy routine. Mr. Logan would flick the reins and shout, "On Donder, on Blitzen!" while Mr. Finch sailed into a rousing rendition of "Rudolph the Red-Nosed Reindeer" on the calliope.

They were a couple of cards, Mr. Logan and Mr. Finch. They played fast and loose.

It usually happened that as the calliope cart proceeded along the parade route, the parade-goers fell in behind it and followed it to the parade's finish line at the Helldorado grounds, where the annual Helldorado rodeo would take place shortly thereafter. The 1957 parade, however, differed strikingly from parades past. When the cart turned onto Main Street, Mr. Logan and Mr. Finch were greeted with mayhem. Riot. A mass hysteria seemed to have seized the crowd. People were screaming, fainting, crying, moaning, trampling each other, and staggering around wholly drunk.

And there were frogs. Everywhere a person looked there were frogs. Frogs splattered in the road, frogs smoking in the popcorn vending machines, frogs hanging from the trees, and frogs that wouldn't have been recognizable as frogs were it not for their shiny green hides.

It was as if God's wrath had been piqued and he'd loosed one of his famous Biblical rains on Pine Bluff. Mr. Finch wondered if someone had stolen sacramental wine, or perhaps sodomized a priest.

It was such an astonishing sight that Mr. Finch neglected his calliope duties. Mr. Logan leapt from the cart, exclaiming, "I'm off to find Martha"—his wife. "The ponies know the way home."

Having no particular damsel-in-distress to rescue—not even, as in Mr. Logan's case, a wrinkled old white woman who turned mean as a poodle in a hatbox at the slightest provocation—Mr. Finch decided that the show must go on. His fingers danced across the calliope keyboard to the tune of "Alexander's Ragtime Band." The cart lurched ahead as the ponies responded to the familiar music. Away they went, over a street slick with vomit and liquefied amphibians.

Mr. Finch had played "Yes We Have No Bananas" and was half-way through "Paddlin' Madeline Home" when he realized that people were following the calliope cart as they had done in years past. The music seemed to be having a soothing effect on them. There was no more rioting in the street. The hysteria had diminished. It gave him an odd feeling to look back and see all those people behind him, walking like zombies, as quiet as suckling infants. He felt like the Pied Piper of Pine Bluff.

They swung past the Helldorado grounds, where the crowd departed from the calliope's wake like a herd of docile cattle. Then the ponies clipped along toward the big barn just beyond the grounds, where they knew they would be freed from the cart and fed.

Once inside the barn, the ponies snorted and stamped their hooves impatiently. Mr. Finch had never released the ponies from their harnesses before, but he was game to try. Just as he was climbing down from the calliope cart's bench to do so, he heard the barn doors slam shut behind him.

Wilda Kolankiewicz stood there with her hands on her hips, naked save for her tiny galvanized bikini bottoms and a pair of rhinestone studded stiletto pumps.

"Save me," Wilda said. It was a command, not a request.

"Um," said Mr. Finch. All of his philosophy, all his knowledge of semantics—indeed, all language—had suddenly fled him.

"I came here to hide when the crowd went wild from all the frogs," Wilda explained. "People were acting so crazy. I thought I might be raped."

Mr. Finch could actually feel his brainwave activity start up again. Her nipples look just like hot pink kazoos! was the first semi-coherent thought in his head.

"As you can see," Wilda went on matter-of-factly, "I've lost all my clothes. Normally I wouldn't mind, but the way things are going today, I'm not about to hop on a horse and do a Lady Godiva number down Main Street."

"Hhwickiphff…" responded the very suave Mr. Finch. He was trying to speak, but his trembling Adam's apple was holding back his words.

She needs a hat! *he thought wildly, followed by an alien interior voice speaking the words Zygote, Organza, and Fern.*

"So will you help me?" *Wilda asked.*

She needs a hat, *Mr. Finch thought once again.*

Mr. Finch descended from the calliope cart bench, which was more difficult than anticipated due to his right leg extending straight out from his body and jerking violently. He lurched over to Wilda muttering nonsense syllables, all the while spastically tipping his hat.

"Mr. Finch, I presume…" *Wilda graciously extended her hand.*

The brown hat was thrust into Wilda's grasp. Mr. Finch shucked the famous brown coat from his shoulders and gave her that, too. Wilda understood. She put on the jacket and tucked her gorgeous red hair up under the hat. But Mr. Finch observed that the disguise was not yet complete.

"Your legs," *he muttered.*

Wilda mistook the observation as an expression of praise, and when Mr. Finch dropped his trousers, she assumed he was overcome with lust. Despite the difference in their age—almost sixty years—Wilda decided to let nature take its course.

As Wilda backed him up against the calliope, Mr. Finch was more than a little surprised to find nature coursing right through him—actually spewing out of him in great big gouts.

18

CAPTAIN NITT-WITT, HIS EXPLANATION OF GOD

Captain Nitt-Witt stood washing dishes in the kitchen sink. Philo stood beside him with a towel, drying the silverware. "I don't have to spell it out for you, do I?" the Captain said. "Your mother got her name from the place where she was conceived—right there on the Lions Club calliope."

"I had no goddamned idea," Philo muttered.

"It's a sweet name—Calliope—but I'm glad everyone doesn't go naming their offspring that way. Otherwise we'd have too many kids running around with names like Chevy and Ford—not to mention all the poor little bastards who would've have to answer to Studebaker."

"Or Sealy Posturepedic," said Philo. He asked what had become of his grandparents.

"Damon passed away before you were born," the Captain told him. "Got stomped by an elk. As for your Grandma Wilda—well, she wasn't up to handling all those wild baby hormones zinging around in her. She splorked out your mother under Brautigan's Oak, then she ran off to become a pirate... or a Zen monk... I'm not sure which."

"Wow. My grandma was a maniac."

"Your grandmother was just dead set on living a more poetic life then most—that's all."

"How do you mean?"

"There's a Yiddish saying that God made man because he loves stories—but I think it's more complicated than that." Captain Nitt-Witt handed Philo the last breakfast plate and sat back down at the table, asking, "Are you up for a little chat about religion?"

"I'd rather learn about fly fishing."

"Some people don't differentiate between the two."

A wet wooden staircase led down to the Rapids of Ego-Loss. As Philo and Captain Nitt-Witt descended it, the roar of waterfalls grew louder in their ears. Cool, misty air rushed up to greet them. When they got to the bottom and entered the cavern, the roar was like a choir of angels. Weird filigrees of light shimmered like lazy lightning on the walls.

Captain Nitt-Witt handed Philo a pair of black rubber waders and told him to go stand on a large flat rock out toward the center of the river. The Captain joined him there moments later wearing a fishing vest over his ratty red robe.

A couple of fly rods quivered in his big-knuckled hands. He showed Philo how to tie on the leaders and flies. Then he demonstrated his casting technique.

"The pole doesn't need to move any further than between ten and two o'clock. The trick is to keep your elbow down and use your wrist. You want everything traveling in a figure eight, with a little bump—there—to keep the fly ahead of the line. See how it's done?"

Captain Nitt-Witt made fly-casting look easy. Philo soon discovered that it isn't.

"Well, hell, nobody gets it right the first time out," the Captain said as he untangled Philo's line from his beard.

Philo was anxious to get on with the lesson. He'd felt a lewd stirring from the moment he first put on the hellish black waders. He wanted to hook a mermaid. He was certain this was possible, in light of everything else he had seen at Nitt-Witt Ridge thus far.

Yes, he could just see some incredibly sexy mermaid vaulting across the river on his line, spraying water from her thrashing thighs and breasts. She's put up a noble fight, Philo was certain, but he would play her well. His line would not snag. His rod would not break. She would land wet and gasping at his feet, wheezing from delicate pink gills. Philo saw himself tenderly bending over to remove the hook from the mermaid's pouting upper lip. Her gratitude would take the shape of some of his cruder sexual imaginings....

But how could any of that happen when he couldn't even get one tiny fucking fly out there?

"Have you ever considered the possibility that God knows your every thought?" Captain Nitt-Witt asked.

Philo was chagrined.

"Every thought in your head," the Captain went on, smiling. "Every vague notion, every passing fancy.... Even those horny daydreams about sullying some fishlady with your trouser trout."

Philo was beyond chagrin. He was considering mortification of the flesh.

"And what if I told you it was okay? That it's just God's way of entertaining Himself. What if I told you that the more colorful or outrageous your thoughts are—as far as God is concerned—the better?"

"I'd say God is one nosy, perverted sonofabitch," said Philo.

"Look at it this way..." Captain Nitt-Witt said. "Before the universe began there was only God—the one, the Absolute, the unknown and Unknowable. To learn about his Oneness, he had to be less than One. So he made Two-ness. Get it? *Duality.* You know—light and dark, earth and air, fire and water, life and death, good and evil, love and hate, oil and vinegar...."

"Okay, I get it," said Philo.

"Well, the truth is, we're all still One with God, but right now we're functioning as a kind of enchanted mirror that tells God stories about His true nature. Or better yet, the universe is one huge novel come to life. It's a simple story, really. It starts out with an explosion in a warehouse. Then some blonde paramecium gets knocked up. The police break in and nail some little guy to a cross.

The first thing you know, everybody on the planet is involved—five or six billion characters in this one book. And the secret identity of every last one of them is none other than the Absolute Author."

"So God made the whole universe and all the people in it just so he could tell Himself stories about Himself?" To express his doubts about that theory, Philo made a face like a sarcastic young salamander.

"I take it you can't work up any sympathy for God's literary ambitions," said the Captain.

"You're saying I'm God, you're God, the guy picking his nose in the supermarket is God. I don't buy it."

"Try to see it from God's point of view. He's everything. He sees everything, hears everything, smells everything, tastes everything, and feels everything. Don't you think he must get tired of seeing himself as some boring middle-management sap with three snotty kids, a bone-crushing mortgage, and a wife who won't sleep with Him?"

"You're telling me God can't get laid?" Philo thought about his own unsuccessful attempt to hook a mermaid.

Captain Nitt-Witt shook his head, saying, "God gets as much pussy as He can stand. That's not my point. My point is, *What will you do with your life to make God's story more interesting?* Will you show him that he's the kind of guy who knows how to enjoy himself? A guy with a quirky sense of humor? A guy who's not afraid to walk on the wild side once in a while? Or will you have the kind of nice, safe, dull-normal life that bores God to tears?"

"If there's one thing I know for sure," said Philo, "it's that I don't want to grow up to be dull-normal."

"That's good, Philo. But I already knew that about you, to tell you the truth. And I'll tell you something else. When you start to get some uniqueness in your life, God takes an interest. He wakes up from his dream a little bit. Helps you along. And that—" Captain Nitt-Witt paused to put his hands on Philo's shoulders, "—that's when things start to get interesting."

19

MICKELODIA, HER FEATHERED PRINCE

The road was full of sleeping snakes. Mickelodia stood among the snakes under pale moonlight. She was cold and alone. Her ankle was inches away from a diamondback rattler at least ten feet long and thicker than a gutter pipe. She didn't dare move for fear of waking it. Every time she took a breath she felt like a broken window.

The broken window appeared in the sky. At that same moment, Mickelodia found an amethyst crystal in her palms. It was weighty and purple. She prayed to it.

An owl's screech tore across the night, announcing a winged prince who swooped heroic through the window and swept Mickelodia up in his feathered arms. She felt her feet leave the ground. A short time later, she was rushing up toward the stars.

The prince was handsome and strong—and he smelled good, too—but all Mickelodia could think was: "How typical. A girl gets herself in trouble and then she just waits around to be saved by some man."

With that critique of her own dream, Mickelodia started to wake up.

Calliope was there to greet her.

"Has anyone ever told you that you snore?"

It took Mickelodia a moment to recall that she was in Pine Bluff, that she had spent the night under a tree and that, yes, that was Philo's mother sitting cross-legged in the grass right in front of her. Calliope hadn't changed much in ten years. Mickelodia made a mental note to ask her if she did anything special to stay looking so young.

"Maybe it's just being outside with the morning dew and all," said Calliope, "but I swear, honey, you snore like a moose."

True camaraderie among men is a rare and difficult thing to achieve. Few males bond and become friends without sharing some sort of Hemingway-styled adventure: alcoholic exploits, marlin fishing, a war, or ball-busting blue-collar work. Men need to see how their friends will hold up in extreme situations. They don't want to be stuck with wimps under pressure.

Friendship among women is based more on intuitive recognition. It's not uncommon for two women who've never met before to be feeling like soul sisters by the end of their first lunch together. Women know a kindred spirit when they meet one. No bullfighting or arm-wrestling required.

It didn't take long for Calliope and Mickelodia to realize they were going to be friends. After establishing that Mickelodia was, indeed, Ned and Pam's daughter, Calliope simply acted as if they had known each other forever. She ordered Mickelodia around with a loopy German accent, informing her that they would be living together from that moment onward. When they got home, Calliope made them both breakfast while explaining the bizarre situation with Harley in the trees. By the time breakfast was over, she and Mickelodia were comparing dress sizes and giddily swapping clothes.

That first morning in Calliope's kitchen, they talked about yoga, homeopathic remedies, and karmic follies. Calliope grew wistful while she rambled on about how much she missed Harley and Philo. Mickelodia listed the many reasons why she would never miss Charlene.

"My mother-in-law!" Calliope exclaimed. "What a witch! I can't believe she had you working as human slave all those years and she never told us!"

"Well, I was," said Mickelodia.

"Oh, don't get me wrong—I believe it all right. That sounds just like her. It just pisses me off, is all. *God!* What nerve!"

"She's not a very nice person."

"She's a fat, vicious, self-centered *cunt!* is what she is…."

Mickelodia was discovering that she and Calliope shared many of the same opinions.

Around noon, when they went outside to do some gardening, Mickelodia felt comfortable enough with Calliope to tell her about the dream she'd had that morning with the snakes and the feathered prince. Calliope, in turn, felt comfortable enough with Mickelodia to interpret the dream for her.

"I thought it might have something to do with my awakening *kundalini*," Mickelodia offered hesitantly.

"Face it, honey," said Calliope, "the princes don't exist. Men are like those snakes half-frozen to death on the road. Sure, they're scary, but we always end up feeling sorry for them—they're so pathetic—plus, they make us horny. So we bring them home, we feed them, we show them a little warmth…. And how do they repay us? They turn around and bite us in the ass!"

Mickelodia grinned. "You gotta love 'em."

"That's the problem: You gotta love 'em."

Calliope vigorously pulled up a few carrots. Mickelodia started doing the same.

"And don't believe that crap about the way to a man's heart is through his stomach," Calliope said. "I'm the best damn cook I know, and my husband would rather cavort with goddamn bluebirds and chipmunks than come home for dinner."

"I just don't get that," said Mickelodia, meaning Harley's whole passion for living in the trees. "It's like he's stuck in some kind of demented Disney movie. *The Swiss Family Marndog.*"

"What's he eat up there?" Calliope wondered aloud. "Nuts and fucking berries?" She stared wildly at Mickelodia and then they both burst out laughing.

After their laughter subsided, Mickelodia asked Calliope how she had fallen in love with Harley.

"Oh God…" Calliope moaned. "The first time I saw him, he was up in a tree with his shirt off. He looked like some kind of Greek god—Zeus, maybe—waving his chainsaw around like it was a fistful of thunderbolts. My first impression was: 'This man is probably very arrogant and very good in bed. I have to meet him.'"

"And was he?"

"Arrogant? Hell, yes! *God,* he pisses me off sometimes…."

"No, I mean—"

"Oh, good in bed? Honey, he was good in bed, in the kitchen, in front of the fireplace, on top of the washing machine…. Hell, he's even good in the goddamn trees."

Mickelodia blushed. She didn't want to, but there was no stopping it. Her cheeks were in flames.

Calliope reached over and tapped her with a carrot. *"You haf never had a man in dot vay, haf you, darlingck?"* she said in her goofy German accent.

"No." Mickelodia looked down at her hands, thinking, *My face must look like the ass on a furious baboon.* Just to be doing something, *anything,* she reached over and jerked up a carrot.

And gasped. The carrot was shaped like a huge penis.

"Whoa! Hang onto that one, honey…" Calliope said. "You might need it."

Calliope decided to tell Mickelodia about the mysteries of love while they were stocking the vegetable pantry.

"Love is a lot like religion," Calliope said. "When you think you've found your soulmate, there's this point where you have to make a leap of faith. If you stand around with your thumb up your butt thinking about it, you don't do it."

"So you think Harley's your soulmate?" Mickelodia asked.

Calliope picked up the penis-shaped carrot and used it to lecture Mickelodia. "Do you think I'd put up with all his crap if he was just some studmonkey? *God!* I can remember the smell of that man's sweat. I can see his face right here in front of me as clear as day. Even after eighteen years of marriage, he can still make my whole body shudder with just one look."

"That bad, huh?"

"That bad, that good. Sometimes Harley makes me swoon. Other times I want to rip out his guts and stomp on 'em."

Calliope fiercely stamped her feet.

"He's my knight in shining armor and the biggest asshole I've ever met. There's times when I'm not sure if I want to screw him or shoot him."

Calliope examined the tip of the waggling penis-carrot as if it was a smoking gun. She set it down.

"I thought love was a lot simpler than that," Mickelodia said. "What makes it so complicated?"

"You have to love like this—" Calliope held out her hands in front of her, palms open—"not like this." She clenched her fists. "You have to let the people you love have their freedom. True loves makes you feel scared and happy at the same time. I guess you could call it *Scappy.*"

"*Scappy...*" Mickelodia tried out the new word. "It kind of makes me think of scabs and crappy birthday songs—but like it."

"Just wait until you feel it. Then tell me how much you like it."

Mickelodia picked up the penis-carrot as if it were a precious talisman. "Do you think I'll ever find my soulmate?" she asked.

"I don't know," Calliope said. "Are you sure you want to?"

Mickelodia decided to give herself some time to think about it.

20

CAPTAIN NITT-WITT, HIS TRAGICOMIC CODPIECE

Weeks passed and Philo continued to be denied the erotic thrill of snagging a mermaid's lip with a Number Two Dang Samuel Gill Buster, but he managed to become fairly adept at fly-casting, nonetheless. On some days, the trout practically leaped into his lap—which was nice, because aside from fishing, Philo wasn't having much fun. Captain Nitt-Witt was making him work like a mule.

Digging trenches, hauling stones, weeding the rose gardens, rebuilding abalone shell walls—there was always some task that needed doing. The hours blurred into a vague recollection of sweat, persistent aches, and bright yellow poundings from the sun. At night, Philo dreamed he was performing even more onerous chores: emptying a lake with a rusty bucket, digging a tunnel through a mountain of granite with nothing but a knitting needle and a plastic spoon. He woke up exhausted, groaning at the prospect of each new day.

Then, subtly, all that hard work began to energize Philo. He started breathing deeper, smelling more acutely, and taking pleasure in sensations like the bite of his shovel against a mound of gravel, or the arc of his sledgehammer's swing. Another long day of physical labor no longer seemed quite so gruesome a curse as it had seemed before.

Philo's body was changing along with his attitude. For the first time in his life, he had obviously defined biceps and pectoral muscles. When he looked in the mirror, Philo saw a body that was closer in appearance to a grown man than a skinny adolescent boy. The transformation was nearly as gratifying for him as that other astonishing transformation of a few years ago, when he reveled over his first public hair. In some ways, it was even better. At least this change wasn't accompanied by hormones wreaking havoc with his voice, causing unpredictable episodes of vocal chord spontaneity that made him sound like a hyena with a bone caught in its throat—usually in the presence of large-bosomed girls.

During his private moments at Nitt-Witt Ridge, Philo began assuming body builder poses in front of windows and still fountain pools—any place with a reflection. The more he thought about it, the more pleased he became with his newfound studliness.

On one particularly hot day in July, Captain Nitt-Witt made Philo take an afternoon off from his labors so they could go on a picnic. The Captain strapped a wicker basket to Philo's back and they hiked through the forest to the edge of a high cliff overlooking the ocean. The wind came off the water in roaring gusts that shook the trees, but when they sat down in a fairy ring of warty red mushrooms, the air was strangely calm. The sound of the thudding waves was no louder than the distant noise inside a conch shell. Philo felt at peace.

"What's for lunch?" he asked, unstrapping the basket and taking a peek inside.

"Seared abalone and tarter sauce sandwiches," said the Captain.

"Sounds gross."

"They used to be Mathilde's favorite."

"Mathilde, your wife?"

"Yeah. We used to come out here all the time. Great spot for whale-watching and... other activities."

Philo bit into a sandwich. It wasn't nearly as bad as he'd anticipated. "What was she like?" he asked with his mouth full of abalone.

"Mathilde? She was one hell of a woman. Smart, gutsy, beautiful... and no sense of balance whatsoever. She was always tripping over things, running into walls. Her knees were constantly scuffed up, just like a little boy's. She slipped and fell so many times getting out of the bathtub that I thought about making a foam-padded shower stall."

"Sounds dangerous."

"Only to herself. We had plans to build a house together, but I swear, she would've killed herself twenty times over working on a place like Nitt-Witt Ridge." Captain Nitt-Witt laughed at some private joke and wiped a tear from his eye.

"How old where you when you got married?" Philo asked.

"Early twenties. Still kids."

"How did you know she was the right one?"

"Oh, I knew.... She was my other self. I knew the minute I set eyes on her. Which is pretty amazing, considering she was a nun."

"A nun?"

"Actually she was a Catholic missionary. Same difference. Her parents were missionaries and it was just something she fell into. Mathilde had been around the world twice by the time she was seventeen. Spoke five or six languages, including Swahili. But all that Catholic dogma was starting to wear on her. She was ready for a change."

"Did her parents like you?"

"They thought I was a madman."

The Captain had met Mathilde and her parents at the Toronto World's Fair, where he was performing in a vaudeville act with a one-legged bicyclist and a three-legged stunt dog—the latter named Tripod Jimmy. The climax of the act, as the Captain explained it, occurred when he feigned heat prostration and fell spread-eagled on the ground, at which time the one-legged bicyclist, pedaling furiously, aimed his front tire directly between the Captain's twitching legs. Just a split-second before certain disaster, the bicyclist executed an amazing tumbling maneuver, flipping the bike completely over the Captain to land safely on the other side. As the crowd cheered this miraculous event, Tripod Jimmy came speeding out of the wings on a fire engine red tricycle, honking the bulb of a silver horn on the handlebars with his teeth. Before Captain Nitt-Witt could get to an upright position, Tripod Jimmy's tricycle inflicted the damage that the one-legged bicyclist had threatened only moments before.

"That must've hurt," said Philo.

"I wore a codpiece," the Captain said. "Still, I worried that all those crashes might be affecting my willie. Fortunately, when me and Mathilde got together, I found that wasn't a problem."

"It must've been weird, making it with a nun."

"It added a little spice, is all. We kept the penguin suit around for laughs. Mathilde liked to wear it into town when she bought my beer and tobacco."

"She sounds like a lot of fun."

"She was. Best damn time of my life."

Captain Nitt-Witt and Philo shared a moment of silence, staring out at the sea.

"I think I'd like to get married someday... maybe," Philo said without thinking. Then he felt instantly embarrassed for being so sincere.

The Captain pulled his silver flask out of his robe and took a long swallow. "Well," he said, squinting his eyes as the drink did a slow burn down his throat, "to my way of thinking, you should know who you are and where you're going before you ask someone to take the trip with you."

"I'm Philo Marndog," Philo said with a confidence he didn't feel.

"That's just a name tag.... What I mean is you should've at least touched the mystery of your own being. Know what you're made of—the spirit of yourself, not the biological meat."

"How do I do that?" Philo asked,

Captain Nitt-Witt passed him the silver flask. "Take a swig of this."

Philo regarded the flask suspiciously. "The last time I did that I hallucinated my ass off."

"It's a different batch this time. Less radish juice, more horse piss."

Philo tipped the flask and took a swallow. He grimaced, then swallowed some more.

"After Mathilde died on me," the Captain said, returning the flask to his pocket, "I turned into a hermit. I guess I already told you this. I was tired of being a man. I didn't have it in me to go on and become another one of those insane apes who worries about his job, his mistress, his taxes, his clothes, his toothaches.... All that stuff seemed petty to me. So I just chucked it—started building the Ridge."

"You must've been pretty depressed," said Philo.

"Sure, but mostly I was indifferent. I wasn't worried about what was going to happen to me anymore. All that energy I'd been frittering away taking care of the details of a normal life was suddenly freed up for me. I was left staring at the one final, non-negotiable truth: We're all beings who are going to die."

"No duh," said Philo, starting to feel just a tad uninhibited.

"Sure, it sounds simple, but here's the kicker: once you accept that fact—and I mean really accept it, live with it and know it every minute of the day—then a crack in the world opens up for you. And you can take all the energy that you were just pissing away before, and you can go through that crack. Freedom and magic and whole other worlds are on the other side, waiting to be discovered. All you have to do is get yourself there."

"I kind of feel like yodeling," Philo said. It was not a joke, just a statement of fact. His pupils were dilating and contracting independently of each other. His nose was running. He seemed on the verge of some prophetic revelation.

"That stuff in the flask," he asked. "What is it, really?"

"This?" Captain Nitt-Witt palmed the flask in his bony hand. A glint of sunlight reflected off it. "This is just transcendental junk food," he scoffed. "But it'll get you through the crack."

"Oh goody…" said Philo, oblivious to the puddle of drool collecting in his lap. He heard the mushrooms singing campfire songs. He sneezed—once, vehemently—then recomposed himself and watched with dignified solemnity as his hair rose up in one solid mass and flapped away toward the ocean like a blonde seabird.

21

PHILO, HIS OWLISH LEAP OF FAITH

He must have passed out. The last thing Philo could remember was his hair abandoning his scalp and flying off into the setting sun. The next thing he knew, it was night and he was flat on his back near a small campfire. The stars looked like fiery pinwheels. The moon was chewing clouds and spitting out fog.

Philo's skull felt like a piñata full of warm, runny macaroni. Every so often, a noiseless explosion went off between his ears, scattering the macaroni to his nether regions. Philo found this sensation quite pleasurable. He stared up at the stars with a goofy smile and willed it to happen again and again.

Suddenly, Captain Nitt-Witt was standing over him shaking a painted tortoise shell rattle and doing some weird Indian-style chanting.

"Go, baby, go!" Philo whooped, feeling no urge for restraint.

The Captain planted his feet on either side of Philo's chest. Philo could see right up his tattered old bathrobe. It looked like he had a Chinese water python jiggling around up there.

"Don't worry if you feel a few sprinkles of rain," said the Captain. "Too many winters have made my plumbing a little leaky, that's all." He shook the rattle to the North and chanted like mad.

"Piss on me, I don't give a damn!" shouted Philo.

"That's quite obliging of you, Philo…" said the Captain as icicles spilled from his nostrils.

Philo thought it strange to see icicles in early August, but certainly no stranger than the sensation of his own ears turning into twin Siamese fighting fish named Professor Smirks and Doctor Bungle. They nipped at each other's tails through the gobs of macaroni substituting for his brain.

Captain Nitt-Witt turned his rattle to the West. He belched fire like a dragon with indigestion. Some of the fire trickled off the end of his beard and ignited Philo's tennis shoes.

The smell of burning rubber inspired a spontaneous burst of poetry from Philo—a celebrational hymn to the joy of living in the manner of William Blake:

"I feel like the cat that ate the tomato!" he shouted. "I got on the dog's pajamas! I'm invisible! I'm fuel-injected! I can make universes and install mini-blinds!"

The Captain turned to the South and shook his rattle. When he chanted, a ferocious windstorm blew out of his mouth and knocked down half the trees in the forest.

"I'm radioactive!" Philo screeched. "I can fart plutonium and give everyone in Kansas an X-ray when I sneeze!"

Captain Nitt-Witt removed the silver flask from his robe and knelt in front of Philo's face.

Philo was shaking his head back and forth, barely aware of him. "Hold me back," he hollered. "I feel like changing the tires on a tractor with my teeth! *WHOA-BOB! WHOO-DANG!*" He tried biting off the Captain's nose.

The Captain took a pull on the flask and blew a fine mist of liquid into Philo's face.

In an instant, Philo was sober.

"Wow, what a rush," he said. "I'm glad that's over."

"Get up," said the Captain. "You need to walk around some."

Captain Nitt-Witt tossed aside his tortoise shell rattle and helped Philo to his feet. They walked out toward the cliff. There was more than enough light from the moon to see by, but Philo was feeling a little dizzy, so he was careful not to get too close to the cliff's edge. Way below them, he could hear the ocean booming against the rocks.

The Captain seemed lost in thought. He was absently gazing at the moonlight dancing on the distant waves. Then he turned and looked at Philo. The look was serious.

"It isn't easy, jumping through the cracks in reality," he said. "But if you confront your fears, you can do it—and you'll never know fear like that again."

Philo felt like a six-year-old having a staring match with the Captain on Halloween again. "I'm not afraid," he said.

"Good. Then jump off this cliff."

Philo glanced over the side of the cliff, as if he was actually, for a split-second, considering it. "Are you crazy?" he asked.

"Jump off the cliff, Philo."

"What the hell for?"

"To find out if you can fly."

Philo scratched himself furiously. His face and chest were breaking out with pinfeathers, but he hadn't noticed them yet.

"I can't fly," he declared. It came out somewhat nasally due to his nose suddenly hardening into an owl's beak.

"Of course you can fly," the Captain said. "Jump."

"No way. It's too high."

"Confront your fears, boy. Jump."

"I'll die if I fucking jump!" Phil squawked.

He tried to run back into the forest. The Captain snagged him by the collar of his shirt. The shirt tore away, revealing long downy feathers growing from Philo's naked arms.

"Look at yourself. The spirit of the Loplop is inside you. You can fly. Now jump."

Philo hugged himself with arms that now looked very much like wings. "I'm too scared!" he cried.

"The water is deep enough to save you, but you're not going to fall. You're going to fly! *Jump!*"

"*NO!*"

With an amazing display of strength for such an old man, the Captain grabbed Philo by the seat of his pants and hurled him off the cliff.

Philo screamed. Panic blazed through him as his feet kicked at nothing. A black expanse of sea rose up to meet his belly. *He was falling!* He stretched out his arms as if he could ward off the crash terror darkness drowning. Strangely, he felt a certain fullness of air beneath his armpits. His headlong plunge turned into a glide. He felt his feathers—*his feathers!*—fluttering in the rush of wind.

He descended in a long flat arc that brought him almost horizontal with the water. He went skimming across the tops of the waves. Then his feet dipped behind him and the water nearly pulled him in. A new surge of panic caused Philo to instinctively hunch his shoulders forward and bring his arms down around him; he almost felt like he was being lifted. He moved easily into the sky as his wings gathered air and pushed against it.

He was flying!

Captain Nitt-Witt stood on the cliff with an ear-to-ear grin.

"Atta boy, Philo!" he shouted. "Flap those wings! *Fly!* I knew you could do it!"

Philo flew up toward the stars, loop-swinging against the cushions of air beneath his wings. He had lost all fear of falling. He looked down and saw the sea below him in the same way that the sky had been above him when he looked from the ground. He could see everything—to his left, Captain Nitt-Witt waving to him from the cliff; to his right, the distant horizon—all without turning his head. He was a bird, a magnificent owlboy.

Never had Philo known air in such cool purity. Never had he been so at home in his own body. He felt the joy of being alive in a way that was entirely new to him. It was a joy that went right down to his wingtips, down to his hollow bones.

He tucked back his wings and went into a dive. The tiger-hum of wind grew louder in his ears. Then he spread his wings wide and caught himself, soaring up into a Ferris wheel-sized loop. He let out an ecstatic yelp. The sky had become his playground.

Captain Nitt-Witt called up to him, laughing, asking how he was doing. There was only one sure way to express how he felt.

Philo started to hoot.

22

CALLIOPE, HER THOUGHTS ON PREGNANCY

Calliope and Mickelodia had settled into a happy routine. In the mornings, they prepared lavish breakfasts: blueberry buckwheat waffles, local fruit in fresh cream, seven grain toast slathered with homemade jams and wildflower honey, and tall frosty glasses of freshly-squeezed orange juice or peppermint iced tea. Then they sat at the kitchen table in the warm morning sunlight and discussed what they could remember of the previous night's dreams.

(The best one so far, they both agreed, had been Calliope's dream about flying in a rocket ship to a distant planet where the little spaceguys who lived there all looked like knee-high-sized penises. According to the etiquette of the planet, to properly introduce herself to the spaceguys Calliope had to sit on them. Each and every one.)

After the breakfast dishes were washed and dried, they went into the living room and sat down to work. Calliope had talked her way into a job as a proofreader for Owlphart Press—a publisher of neo-surrealist fiction based in Pine Bluff. They gave her galley proofs every Thursday, which she and Mickelodia corrected over the week and then returned the following Thursday. The pay was modest, but it was enough to cover their needs without having to rely on Harley.

Around noon, they did a little gardening and went into town to run errands. Then more proofreading—or if the weather was nice, a trip to the beach.

In the evenings, after a vegetarian dinner, Calliope led Mickelodia on a moonlit hikes through the woods near the house.

They walked until they were satisfied they had burned off any evil extra calories that lurked on their bodies, waiting to mutate into lumpy tapestries of fat. When they got home, they usually made popcorn and settled in to watch some videotapes.

Sometimes they had friends over and sometimes they babysat the children of those friends.

It was a pleasant but unremarkable life.

On the night of Philo's ecstatic owlboy transfiguration, Calliope and Mickelodia were out on their usual evening hike. They had been discussing the deeply ingrained pettiness of certain people who belonged to the Pine Bluff Food Co-op when, echoing from across the distance, they heard Philo's ecstatic owlboy yelp.

Calliope grabbed Mickelodia's arm. "God, what's that?" she said with a feigned sense of terror. "Could it be... an owl with a hernia?"

They both stopped to listen. Another ecstatic yelp echoed toward them from the direction of the sea.

"Do albatrosses have orgasms?" Mickelodia asked.

"You know what?" Calliope said excitedly. "That's exactly the sound Philo made when he was born."

"Didn't he cry?"

"No! It was so weird! There I was, squatting next to the kitchen table, trying to push this gigantic *thing* out of me into Harley's hands. All of a sudden I knew it was happening. My brain got out of the way and my body just did it. Three, maybe four really huge pushes—it's like taking the shit of your life—and *BOOSH!*—a baby came out. Harley looked up at me and said, 'Hey, it's a boy!' and that baby just started making the most joyful noise...."

"Aw, how sweet," said Mickelodia, some deep part inside her twitching sympathetically.

"You don't know that half of it, honey. When Harley put that baby in my arms, I fell in love, like that." Calliope snapped her fingers. "All during my pregnancy, I felt like I was carrying around this weird alien creature that was making me fat and crazy and embarrassing the hell out of me. But once I saw him—*WHAM!*—instant love."

"What was embarrassing about it?" Mickelodia asked. "I think pregnant women are beautiful.

Calliope rolled her eyes. "Oh, sure. I was just gorgeous—a real peach. Nobody told me about the hormonal insanity. The constantly having to pee...." She started to get agitated. *"God!* You know what? When I gave birth, I ripped myself from poozle to pucker. I had to have stitches up my butt that made me live in mortal fear of taking a crap for a month!"

Mickelodia saw through the act. "And I bet you'd do it all again" she said.

"In a heartbeat." Calliope calmed down instantly. "Having a baby really puts you in touch with what life's all about. I think that's why men are always off having wars, starting religions, and living in trees. They can't have babies."

"What if you got pregnant again? Do you think Harley would come home?" Mickelodia knew from previous conversations that Calliope had been considering it.

"I don't know..." Calliope sighed. "Harley's been acting so strange lately, sometimes I think the only way to straighten him out would be to get *him* pregnant."

Calliope held her hands out in front of her, pantomiming a midwife, or perhaps an NFL quarterback. "That's right, Harley," she purred, "take nice, slow, steady breaths. That's it, slow and steady...." Then she barked: "Now push, Harley! *Push,* you big stud! *PUUUSSSSSSHHH!"*

☐ ☐ ☐ ☐ ☐ ☐ ☐ ☐ ☐

Philo flew right over Mickelodia and his mother on silent golden wings. He had spied them from afar, two tiny figures laughing in the tall grass of a zebra meadow. He'd considered coming in for a landing, but decided against it. He really wanted to show off his new powers of flight, but he was afraid his appearance would only scare his mother and the red-haired girl walking with her. His beak had made it all but impossible for him to speak. Not only wouldn't his mother be able to recognize him, worse, she'd probably equate him with one of those bizarre and sinister flukes of nature like Bigfoot or the Abominable Snowman. She loved reading trashy supermarket tabloids about three-headed babies, ice cream diets, and alien hairdressers. He could already see the headline: **OWLBOY ATTACKS PINE BLUFF MOM!**

Too bad she didn't have a camera with her. If his mom could get a photo credit of her very own in the *National Enquirer*, Philo thought it almost might be worth the fright.

23

HARLEY, HIS SQUIRRELLY EXISTENTIAL MUSINGS

Harley was sprawled on his back, suspended in a nest of ropes and tree climber's gear in the boughs of an old sycamore tree. The moon shone pale on his gaunt, sweaty face. His eyes were darting back and forth in R.E.M. sleep. He was almost grimacing.

The shadow of his flying son passed over him, but Harley was too deep in his own dreams to notice.

He was dreaming of his mother. She was trying to shoot him with a deer rifle—a .22 Hornet that his father had owned, to be precise. Harley was running away from her through a forest of young pines and she was running after him, laughing. She seemed to be having some trouble working the rifle's bolt. Then she fired once and Harley felt the angry energy of the bullet as it whizzed past his ear.

There was an old barn up ahead. Harley was running so fast that he was able to leap on the top strand of a barbed wire fence and launch himself—slingshot style—right up onto the barn's roof. His mother fired another shot. Dust and old shingles exploded to his left. He kept running. Shingles slid out from under his feet. It was like trying to run up a down escalator. Finally—out of breath—he reached the top. His mother fired again, missing him by inches. Harley just stood there on the ridge, frozen. He couldn't believe mother was doing this. She slid another bullet into the rifle's chamber. This time she squinted and aimed with the scope.

Harley wanted to run someplace higher and further, but there was no place left to go.

□ □ □ □ □ □ □ □ □

For months, Harley had been thinking deeply. He wanted to clear away all the blame and guilt and anger that was keeping him from leading an authentic life. Whenever he had an insight that seemed especially meaningful or profound, he wrote it down on a postcard in tiny, looping handwriting that looked like forget-me-nots. He later stashed the postcards in abandoned squirrel hollows for posterity.

Lately, he'd been giving a lot of thought to his relationship with his mother. One of the reasons Harley had married Calliope was that he knew she would be a good mother to their children. His own mother, with her unpredictable explosions of rage, had destroyed whatever closeness there might have been between them by the time he was five. It didn't help that she had routinely beaten him with a pancake spatula, and once, duct-taped his head to a portable black and white television for no good reason. When Harley thought back on his childhood, all he could recall were moments of uneasy truce between them. There was never any love. In fact, he had become convinced, quite young, that his mother despised him.

Charlene had rationalized her outbursts to other adults. She claimed she had migraine headaches and Harley, the wicked boy, pushed her past her limits. But Harley was usually just minding his own business when she went after him. He would be playing in the backyard with his friends, for instance, and suddenly his mother would come marching out of the house with murder in her eyes and the dreaded spatula in her hand, screaming that they were "playing too loud." And Harley would get whacked right in front of his little buddies.

All through school, he had a reputation for having The Meanest Mom in Pine Bluff. He couldn't wait to grow up so he wouldn't have to deal with her anymore.

□ □ □ □ □ □ □ □ □

As a child, Harley had blamed his own actions for his mother's violence. As an adult, he knew better. He speculated on the psychological and biochemical factors that might have been at the bottom of his mother's dysfunctional behavior.

Maybe the migraines were real.... She certainly took enough painkillers for them. Her medicine cabinet had always been full of Darvon, Percoden, and codeine. She'd placed so much importance on these drugs that Harley, as a small boy, memorized their names and often whispered them to himself before he went to sleep. His later obsession with psychopharmacology probably stemmed from there.

She also took prednisone—for her skin rashes—in such huge doses that it was dangerous to her health. Not only was prednisone hard on the liver and kidneys, but at the dosage level his mother had been taking it at—*for years*—it could also provoke psychotic reactions.

So maybe ol' Charlene had been a borderline psychotic all that time.

Who knows?

Harley could forgive his mother a lot by writing it off to bad chemistry, but the one thing he couldn't forgive her for was the death of his father. She had been openly having an affair. She was practically writing about it in the local newspaper, according to some folks in town Harley talked to later. But that by itself shouldn't have been enough to cause his father to commit suicide. It was probably the daily nagging and bitching that wore him down.

Imagine being a miner, going down in a hole every day so you never see the sun, working like some overgrown gopher, and then coming home to Charlene's hostility. She's already spent all the money you earned and now she's humping some yellow journalist right under your nose. Why do you put up with it?

That was the question Harley couldn't get around: *Why did his father put up with it?* Why did he marry Charlene in the first place? Why did he let her boss him around? Why did he allow her to beat his only son? Instead of killing himself, why not just get a divorce?

Harley had to conclude that his father, in his own passive way, was just as screwed up as his mother. And that was hard for him to admit, because he'd really loved his father. But it had to be said:

My dad was a wimp.

On the back of a postcard with a picture of a well-muscled young man shown from the neck down clutching a naked newborn baby to his chest, Harley wrote:

```
i was twelve
when you exploded yourself
in the turnips and dry summer grass
at the edge of our vision
the crows dropped like mud
from a blackwater sky to pick you apart
sucking marrow from your long bones
i found a dozen white seeds
scattered on my windowsill
it was years before i could admit
they were your own far flung teeth
i know the woman you married
i know the hours you spent hacking
the ground to dust in the same dark hole
must not have seemed worth the effort
but there were so many people
you never knew who only know you
as a torn black and white photo
in a half-empty scrapbook
on a shelf next to our old shoes
```

After his father died, the only place where Harley ever felt safe was in the woods. Somewhere in the back of his mind, he knew that if his mother came after him out there, he could always climb a tree. Charlene was too fat to climb very high.

Harley supposed that was why he had such a love for being in the trees as an adult. In the trees he was free. No worries, no anxieties—just him and his tree climbing gear, achieving Oneness with Nature.

He knew his family thought he was abandoning them, just as his own father had abandoned him. But it wasn't like that. He loved Calliope and Philo. He tried to look after them as best as he could. There were just some things he had to work through on his own.

Because he was blanking out.

He was becoming more and more a rooster.

And he was starting to worry that some of his mother's violence was also in him.

24

VIC TIM, HIS RIBALD HAIR SALOON

ourists loved to walk the streets of Pine Bluff. Everything was so tree-lined and quaint. Wilfred Logan's General Store enchanted everybody with its sagging porch, its rusty old Coca-Cola signs, and its weathered timbers. It was so charmingly dilapidated that it seemed on the verge of sliding backward into the creek. A few steps beyond, the delicious smells of simmering garlic and curries wafted into the air from the Thai and Indonesian dishes served on the vine-covered patio of Shana's Restaurant. Next door to Shana's, Mr. Finch's faded butter-yellow Victorian home stood behind a tangle of brambles and tall, statesman-like elms. Past the Finch house, past the volunteer fire department, there was a structure out of the Old West, complete with hitching posts and bullet-spattered double doors. Painted on the front windows in gold gilt lettering, the passing tourist could read: *VIC TIM'S HAIR SALOON; Where Pine Bluff comes to dye.*

Victor Tim, and his hair saloon partner, Peter-Jon DeVrode, had met at the University of California at Santa Barbara, where they'd been the only two Dutch-Indonesian freshman majoring in chemical engineering. They got to know each other through study groups and found they shared mutual passions for cleanliness, hikes through pine forests, and laying girls.

One weekend, Victor invited Peter-Jon along for a drive up the coast to see his Aunt Shana in Pine Bluff. They bathed early in the morning and then made themselves snug in the red vinyl seats of Victor's 1963 Renault Caravelle convertible. The Renault (turquoise exterior, plucky four-cylinder rear engine) whisked

Peter-Jon and Victor up Highway 1 with the ocean breeze raking through their stylish black hair.

They were happy then, just two carefree Dutch-Indonesians on the loose in California, both of them exuding hubris and the smell of hot lathered soap.

When they arrived in Pine Bluff, Victor and Peter-Jon somehow knew they had found their spiritual home. The town was clean and surrounded by Monterey Pines. The women—New Age hippies and rich yuppie tourists—were all quite fabulous. That night, by chance, Victor and Peter-Jon watched Warren Beatty balling his brains out in *Shampoo* on Shana's VCR—and they saw their future. The next week, back in Santa Barbara, they both enrolled in beauty school.

Their plan was to open a beauty salon in Pine Bluff and pretend to be homosexuals. In this way, they could make a pile of money, avoid all further courses in chemical engineering, and lay every one of their beautiful clients. The faggotry would be a perfect cover. If a husband or boyfriend suspected them, they would cheerfully offer to suck his dick.

Shana bankrolled them. Her restaurant was doing so well that she didn't even need to think about it twice. That was over six years ago. The profits in the first year were slim—Victor and Peter-Jon's shampooing to screwing ratio was in need of some fine tuning—but Vic Tim's Hair Saloon had been a raving success ever since.

"Make me look young, Vic."

It was the standard request. On this occasion it came from a platinum blonde of about fifty, who dressed and acted as if she was twenty: Vanessa. Victor had reluctantly bedded her a few months ago, only to find that she had an amazing, muscular vagina that kept him sexually enthralled for hours. He had grown quite fond of Vanessa. He almost considered her a friend.

Victor adjusted the blue vinyl apron beneath Vanessa's chin, caressing the tight skin along her jaw-line as he did so. "Don't worry, Vanessa," he said, "you'll never grow old. When you start to show your age, just get another facelift and you'll be fine."

Vanessa's brown spaniel eyes widened in surprise. "What do you mean, *another facelift?* I've never had a facelift in my life!"

Peter-Jon minced by. He had initially affected mincing to support his gay charade, but now he did it without thinking. He liked to mince.

Victor blew a kiss in his direction. "Peter-Jon, suggest a new hairstyle to Mrs. Buckley. Those ringlets make her look like an electrocuted poodle."

"I rather like the effect myself," Peter-Jon replied in the bitchy tone he saved for the hair saloon. "It makes me think of Shirley Temple diddling herself with a Tesla coil."

They both shared a wicked little laugh over that one.

"You don't think I believed the story about the car wreck," Victor said confidentially to Vanessa.

"I hit my chin on the dash."

Victor imitated Vanessa's girlish whine: "The car's okay, but I bruised my face."

"Right!" Vanessa sat up in her chair, feigning indignation.

Victor mimicked her ruthlessly: "—And at the same time, my wrinkles just happened to disappear!" He poked his fingers into his cheeks and gave her a Shirley Temple grin.

Quietly—"I look the same to me," Vanessa said, making a show of examining herself in the mirror.

"Why lie, Vanessa? So you had a facelift. It worked. You look fabulous."

Vanessa slumped. "Oh, god… you knew the whole time?"

"Your hairdresser always knows for sure."

"I can't believe this. I'm mortified."

"Why?" Victor started trimming her hair.

"Well, what if you went in for an operation to get a bigger penis? Would you want everyone to know?"

Victor's scissors snipped away at the ends of her hair in a flurry. In contrast, his voice was slow and cadenced: "Vanessa, I was in a car wreck...."

She laughed.

"The car's okay, but I bruised my prick."

Vanessa stared, agog, at Victor's crotch. She pretended to grasp an enormous invisible dick.

"Omigod! It's huge!" she cried.

Victor admired himself in the mirror, legs splayed and pelvis thrust forward like a bawdy pirate. Arms across his chest, he said manfully: "I look the same to me."

Vanessa bent over laughing. It was then that she noticed the chickens.

There was a tremendous crash. The air in the hair saloon was suddenly clouded with plaster dust and flapping poultry. A harsh, metallic voice boomed out:

"Sinners and lazybums! The lord God saith unto thee: 'Ye are a vain and snooty-faced people.'"

Victor, stunned, thought to himself, *The Jehovah's Witnesses usually knock first....*

"Ye who would forsake His Glory to worship at the altar of Vidal Sassoon..." the metallic voice thundered, "ye are no more than an abomination wafting in the back of the Lord thy God's blindingly white underpants!"

Peter-Jon, over in a corner, squeaked out: "Amen!"

A massive figure appeared out of the plaster dust fog. It was part machine, part Tyrannosaurus Rex... and part rooster.

A variety of wickedly gleaming kitchen implements hung off a utility belt around the creature's hips. He unsheathed a four-foot long Sunbeam electric carving knife and brandished it in the air.

"Reprobates! Jezebels! Foul homos!"

Vanessa observed the creature speaking through a mechanical beak that was out of sync with the words, like a poorly dubbed Japanese horror movie.

"The Almighty Lord saith: 'I shall smite your shopping malls, your salad bars, and your precious hair saloons. For I am a wildly jealous God, and I'm completely fed up with this wickedness!'"

With that, the electric carving knife came down and sawed off Vanessa's head.

25

ZEPHYR ZENDADA, HIS LIFE AND HIGH TIMES

Zephyr Zendada was a person who had given up all pretense of not being a fool. He thought of himself as a holy fool, actually—one of God's jesters. He had once been an extremely serious young man, but seriousness had backfired on him. Seriousness had led him to irony, and irony had led him to mind-paralyzing paradoxes. Now he was quite happy to live those paradoxes. He considered himself a jilted narcissist, a spiritual hedonist, a pragmatic mystic, a self-renouncing egomaniac. He was at once the secret hero and biggest jackass of the universe.

In short, he was a Sensuous Hermit.

He was a small, skinny, hairy man prone to wearing tie-dyed Grateful Dead T-shirts and cut-off shorts. His forehead was high and what little hair remained above it was long and straggly. He had a bushy beard the shade and consistency of steel wool left to rust under a leaky kitchen sink. When he smiled, which was often, he exhibited the yellowed buckteeth of some amiable rodent.

Some people thought he looked like Jesus, but only if he kept his mouth shut.

Zephyr lived in an orange 1979 Dodge Ramcharger four-wheel drive pickup outfitted with a wooden camper shell that had stained glass windows and a pointed shake roof with a stovepipe coming out of it. The camper gave the Ramcharger some cornering problems, but it was Zephyr's home and over the years he had gotten used to driving slow.

He spent his time touring the national parks and wilderness areas of the western United States. He had no permanent address—just a post office box in Pine Bluff where he picked up his mail two or three times a year.

There was nothing ever pending in Zephyr's life, so he was never in a hurry to get anywhere. He had a loathing of schedules, commitments, and alarm clocks. He allowed the weather and his own peculiar whims to dictate the course of his travels. He liked to tell people he was on The Road to Nowhere. He acted the part of a latter-day Henry David Thoreau. He had no ties to any home, land, or people. What simple things he needed were all contained within his camper. He was free!

He often neglected to tell people that he'd started a hippie candlestick factory back in the sixties that he'd sold for about half a million dollars back in 1971.

The interior of Zephyr's camper was furnished in early Zen Lunatic: simple pine bookcases (featuring the collected works of Carlos Castaneda, Alan Watts, Sri Aurobindo, Chuang Tzu, and Gurdjieff), plain white sheets, a propane stove, and a small refrigerator with a scene of nude woodland fairy-women painted on its door. Quartz crystals dangled from the ceiling on copper wires, casting rainbow patterns of light on the walls. Secure in bins up near the skylights, rare Ecuadorian bonsai papaya trees sprouted with sticky purple buds.

Two puffs of the papaya buds through the nourishing tubes of Zephyr's streamlined, glass-walled, water-cooled, faux-Indian hookah and you would see the invisible geckos on the inside of your eyeballs.

Three puffs and you either achieved Oneness with the Absolute or went stark raving insane. Barking-at-the-moon, sticking-forks-in-your-own-gonads, seeing-Richard-Nixon-talking-to-Mahatma-Gandhi-at-the-Dairy-Queen-insane. Not the nice kind of insane, like William Blake.

Zephyr always took three puffs, but he was careful to send up a little prayer to Yogananda and W.C. Fields beforehand, asking for a metaphysical wink and a nod.

It was in this altered state of consciousness—watched over by mystic soul-emanations of swami and comic—that Zephyr rolled into Pine Bluff to pick up his mail once more.

It was a Tuesday, and Tuesday was Transvestite Day. Zephyr was wearing a dress. It was a classic muumuu, as worn by natives of small tropical islands where volcanoes vomit fire and cover everything with lava to periodically purge the land of bad taste. It was made of a shiny rayon material with a pattern of hibiscus blooms and crazed toucans. It was ample enough for an adolescent hippopotamus to wear with comfort, but only if that same creature had been blind since birth.

Zephyr wanted to transcend all gender distinctions, forget about the categories of male and female, and simply see people as human beings. He found that wearing a dress once a week gave him an edge.

Plus, the silk panties felt really great.

He pulled up in front of Vic Tim's Hair Saloon, which was just across the street from the post office. Zephyr decided to pop in on his old friend Victor to see what he thought of the outfit—and maybe get himself a perm.

"Victor!" Zephyr shouted, approaching the hair saloon's double doors like a faggy gunslinger. "Ol' Zephyr Zendada just rode into town, and he's got him some split-ends to settle with you!"

From behind the double doors, a low voice said: "Victor's gone. The Lord hath dubbed me Calydon…. Have a seat."

A salon chair, with the Space-Age-looking hair dryer still attached, exploded through the doorway, smashing both doors to smithereens. Zephyr caught the chair with his chest and stumbled backward to thump his head on the side of his truck.

Fortunately, he was so relaxed that he wasn't hurt. Another benefit of his healthful papaya buds was that three puffs turned a person's bones to jalapeño jelly.

A large figure loomed in the splintered doorway.

"Calydon!" Zephyr said, adjusting the salon chair in his lap. "What the hell kinda name is that for a giant chrome rooster who looks like he shops at K-Mart and's into kinky sex?"

Calydon stepped onto the sidewalk, jangling kitchenware from his utility belt. He was insulted. Not one of his gleaning chrome implements of death had been bought from K-Mart. He had purchased everything from quality mail-order catalogues.

"Who art thou to speak?" Calydon sneered. "A queer man in a dress."

"I'm a stockbroker on a holiday, dipshit."

Calydon's black cloak billowed out behind him, and in an instant his scaly, reptilian hand was grasping Zephyr's throat.

"The Lord hath no use for smart-mouths and transvestites," said a very peeved Calydon.

Zephyr wheezed through his constricted esophagus: "Not even if they kin type?"

With a horrible crow, Calydon threw Zephyr over the roof of the Ramcharger's camper. He then proceeded to demolish the camper with his hydraulically-assisted fists.

By all rights, Zephyr should have been dead with a broken neck. Instead, he just kind of stretched. His height increased by almost four inches—a new mystery for chiropractors everywhere.

Zephyr scrambled to his feet. He quietly lifted his acoustic guitar off the front seat of his truck, then snuck around and used it to whomp Calydon on the backside of the head.

Skplang! Calydon's chrome rooster head rang like the gong in a Buddhist Temple.

Nam-myoho-renge-kyo, buddy, thought Zephyr. He tried to get a handle on his Buddhist non-attachment to all worldly things. But what he ended up saying, quite indignantly, was, "You're wreckin' my house, you dumb cock!"

Calydon clutched his still-ringing head. "God will smite you with death for that, hippie scum," he thundered.

But Zephyr was already a block away. He turned to stick out his tongue and waggle his hands at his ears. Then he lifted his dress and scampered away on bare feet.

Calydon would just have to smite him another day.

26

MICKELODIA, HER IMPATIENCE WITH SUFFERING

Calliope and Mickelodia were catching up on their reading while sunning themselves in matching string bikinis at Moonstone Beach. A recent high tide had piled golden-green seaweed all along the high-tide line. The seaweed, baking in the hot sun, had attracted sand fleas and other small insects. Every now and then, Mickelodia and Calliope lifted their legs up in the air and pedaled invisible bicycles in an attempt to keep the bothersome insects away.

"What are these things?" asked an annoyed Mickelodia. "Sand fleas? Seaweed flies?"

"I don't know what they're called," Calliope replied. "They sure are obnoxious little critters, though, aren't they?"

Mickelodia slapped at her slim ankles. She had worked up an absolutely incredible pout. "I hate 'em," she declared. "Why did God ever make things like flies in the first place? I mean, they land in shit, they carry disease…. They don't serve any real purpose. It's not like they pollinate flowers or anything."

"Maybe they're here just to piss us off," Calliope suggested darkly.

"Yeah, and why is that? Why all the bugs and germs? Why does everything born have to suffer and die? Why are there starving babies Somalia?"

"Whoa… we just went from seaweed flies to starving babies. That's pretty big jump there, girl."

"Well, so what?" Mickelodia pedaled her invisible Schwinn. "You and I both know the Buddhists say 'Life is suffering.' But I want to know why. Why does it have to be that way?"

Calliope considered the question. Several frivolous answers immediately leapt to mind, but she decided she'd try to answer thoughtfully:

"I think we learn things from suffering," she said.

Mickelodia's eyes flashed. "So you'd perpetuate wars, rape, pestilence, murder, and starvation just because they teach you things? Why don't you learn to use the fucking library?!"

Calliope laughed. "What is this, Mick? Are we having a little PMS today?"

"I'm serious!"

"So am I! All pain is growing pain."

"What a bunch of crap."

"Don't you get it? The mind is a mirror. Everything we hope for or fear we attract into our lives. And every problem we run into has a window for our growth."

Mickelodia swatted the air with a paperback copy of the *Bhagavad-Gita* and said, "Oh, like I was really hoping for these flies...."

"It's right there in your book," Calliope said. She had been skimming through it earlier. "It says, 'Man is made by his belief. As he believes, so he is.'"

"So I believe in flies...."

"Look: everything's an illusion in this world. Death, pain, suffering, flies—they're all illusions. The only thing real is what happens in our minds."

Mickelodia picked up a strand of seaweed and swung it like a whip. It made a very satisfying snap against Calliope's thigh.

"Ow! You bitch!"

"Was that an illusion?" Mickelodia asked her.

Calliope rubbed the welt rising in a pink line across her leg. "I guess I was asking for that one," she said.

"Damn straight you were." Assuming the demeanor of a stern schoolmistress, Mickelodia shook a finger at her and said, "We'll have no more metaphysical bullshit out of you today, Miss Calliope Marndog, thank you very much."

□ □ □ □ □ □ □ □ □

Calliope and Mickelodia had elaborate plans for the coming Helldorado Parade. Among other things, they had decided to build a float.

They had found corporate sponsorship for the project by way of a tuna cannery executive who owned a vacation home in Pine Bluff. After a week-long ordeal with tissue paper and chicken wire on the back of a borrowed flatbed truck, the end result was a thirty foot long movable fish wearing round-rimmed spectacles and a black mortarboard on its head. It was supposed to be Charlie the Tuna—the legendary figure from cartoon advertising campaigns of years past. Calliope and Mickelodia, dressed as chickens, intended to appear as Charlie's Chicken-of-the-Sea consorts.

Why this idea appealed to them neither one could say, but it had gotten to the point where if either of them so much as hummed the Chicken-of-the-Sea jingle, they both collapsed into helpless fits of laughter.

Certain women can put up with a pleasant but unremarkable life for only so long.

Mickelodia nearly fulfilled Calliope's need for companionship, but she wasn't equipped to satisfy Calliope's more wild-assed longings. Harley still had his uses.

Every once in a while—usually on nights when the red wine and metaphysical bullshit had flowed especially freely—Calliope would put on something sexy and go out into the woods to find her husband after Mickelodia had fallen asleep.

Harley had a keen intuition for when Calliope was out prowling on those nights. Knowing what was good for him, he always went to her as fast as the trees would allow.

On one such night, Calliope found Harley sitting at the top of a sturdy toyon shrub, making a nest from strands of his own misery.

"Why the long face, poopsie?" Calliope asked, lit up with cheap merlot.

Harley sighed. "I've just been thinking a lot, I guess."

"Well, cheer up. Your filthy-minded love goddess is here."

"I don't know if I'm in the mood tonight, Clippy."

Calliope bristled. Her drunkenness had put her on that weird borderline between frisky good cheer and belligerence. Harley turning her down for sex and calling her Clippy had nudged her over toward the belligerent side.

"You're not in the mood for much these days, are you?" she snapped.

"What's that supposed to mean?"

"You know what I mean."

"No, I don't." A touch of exasperation was showing through Harley's gloom.

"You never do anything with me anymore," Calliope said, wishing now that she'd worn something more than just a flimsy, see-through white negligee. "I've been building a float for the past week! I'll bet you didn't even know that, did you?"

"A float? What for?"

"I'm going to be in the Helldorado Parade, you moron! And, damnit, you better be there to see it!"

"You know I hate being around all those tourists...."

"Harley!" Calliope shouted.

"What?"

"There *is* such a word as Divorce."

Even in the moonlight, Calliope could see the color drain from Harley's face. It made her feel powerful, but also a little scared.

"Please don't ever say that..." Harley whispered.

"This monkeyman act of yours has gone on long enough. You better hurry up and get over whatever it is you're going through, or you might not have a wife when you get back on the ground."

Harley didn't say anything. But the way he looked chilled Calliope deep inside. Now she was *really* scared.

"There're trees all along Main Street," she said, backpedaling, wanting to make things easier for him. "Maybe you could watch us from one of those."

"Okay," said Harley. "I promise I'll be there."

"You'd better be."

Calliope walked back toward the house—spooked, but proud of herself for not completely backing down.

Sometimes it took balls of steel to have a husband.

27

CALLIOPE, HER HELLDORADO BABEHOOD

A sleazy circus magic always stole over Pine Bluff on the morning of the Helldorado Parade. At dawn, the traditional rooster crows were supplemented with clanging cowbells and the bleats of abused trumpets. Everyone in town got out of bed early, most of them with an unwholesome sense of anticipation, knowing they would be getting out of tomorrow's bed much later, if at all.

Shriners everywhere donned their fezzes and inspected the fuel and oil levels in their go-carts with the solemnity of jet fighter mechanics. The Rotarians garbed themselves in papier-mâché breastplates, women's wigs, and pointy plastic hats with diminutive moose antlers attached. The hour had arrived for them to be Vikings and swear at the tourists in fake Swedish.

Over at the rodeo grounds, the air was thick with smells of burning sausages and blueberry waffles from the Lion's Club Annual Helldorado Breakfast. Within the shabby confines of Wilfred Lyon's General Store, the local cowboys were stocking up on whiskey and prophylactics. As the time for the parade drew near, everyone—locals and tourists alike—busied themselves setting up lawn chairs along the sidewalks of Main Street.

Calydon's rampage was the talk of the town. Little else was being discussed. It was far and away the most horrific event in Pine Bluff's history. Six people dead—and Handsome Hank the mailman and poor old Mrs. Andersen still missing. The city council had debated a proposal to cancel the Helldorado Parade, but local business owners had objected. Many of them relied on the tourist income generated by the event to carry them through the lean winter months ahead.

A brief exchange—typical of most of the conversations along Main Street that day—took place between Philo's Aunt Virginia and Uncle Balmeister as they settled into their matching orange plastic rattan lawn chairs with their matching Hawaiian shirts, matching shorts, matching sunglasses, and matching piña coladas:

"Did you hear that man talking about the hair salon murders?" Virginia inquired.

Balmeister tapped his hearing aid. "Virginia, I can barely hear you, much less some jackass spreading gossip twenty yards away."

Virginia continued, undaunted. "Four women and two homos—all dead. They were thinking of canceling the parade."

"That would've been bad for business. Shop owners would've been sore as hell." Balmeister bent forward, groaning, to pat the head of his faithful basset hound, Theotis, who was looking up at him respectfully, albeit uncomprehendingly.

"Someone said a giant rooster did it," said Virginia, pursing her lips in disapproval.

"I don't doubt it for a second..." Balmeister sighed, leaning back in his chair with a luxuriant air of weariness.

"Bal, you're drunk."

"I don't doubt it for a second...."

"I hope you're not going to embarrass me in front of Harley and Calliope."

"I wont be giving Philo anymore exploding hamsters, if that's what you mean." Balmeister patted his flabby stomach and dislodged a moist belch. Theotis snapped at it as if his master had just spit up a butterfly.

The Chicken-of-the-Sea float was idling on Bridge Street next to the old bank building, waiting its turn in line. Calliope and Mickelodia were perched on the bow, in front of Charlie the Tuna's gaping mouth, watching the start of the parade pass in front of them. They were wearing their feathery white chicken costumes, but the chicken heads themselves were lying lifeless at their feet. Seen from a distance, it looked as if both chickens had suffered bloodless decapitations—and now they were standing around with their exposed esophagi, talking about the weather.

The float carrying the Helldorado Queen and her court went by. It depicted a snowy fairytale paradise littered with beer cans and snowmobiles. Donna Portada-Rupert, the new queen, stood at the center of it all like a monument, seeming quite pleased with her twinkly crown and her torpedo-like enhooterment.

"I know for a fact those boobs are fake," Calliope said.

"Shouldn't she be disqualified?" Mickelodia asked in a tone of innocence and wonder.

"Around here it doesn't matter. Besides, she's a nice girl. Even if she *did* blow all the judges."

"You almost sound jealous."

"*Moi?* Jealous?" Calliope clutched her breast with her stubby chicken wings. "Okay, sure, I've always wanted to be one of those awesome Helldorado babes. Stand up in front of a bunch of drunks with hard-ons and flash my titties. I admit it, *darlingck*—" she suddenly shifted into her loopy German accent—*"I vant to be a famous sex goddess!"*

"It *is* kind of demeaning...."

"No more than wearing a chicken suit. *God,* I'm so thrilled!" Calliope trilled. She tried to hug Mickelodia, but their costumes got in the way. "I didn't think anyone but Philo would have the balls to dress up as a chicken with me."

"Do you think Philo will be here today?" Mickelodia still hadn't met him.

"He'd better be." Calliope said, squinting her eyes as if she was auditioning for a spaghetti western. "If he's not, I'm gonna go slap that Captain Nitt-Witt around some—I don't care how old he is."

"What's he look like?"

"Philo? Oh God, he's such a handsome kid. No wait—a handsome *Young Man.* He's got a real cute tush on him, too."

"Really?"

"Yeah." Calliope could see Mickelodia's interest. "Y'know, now that I think about it, you two might make a sweet couple."

"Soulmate material, maybe?"

"I don't know. If he is, you'll know when you meet him."

Calliope smiled—a little anxiously, Mickelodia thought. They both bent over to pick up their chicken heads as the float shuddered and started rolling toward the Main Street.

"Now let's go find that dim-bulb soulmate of mine," Calliope said, donning her chicken head. "It's time to see if he's got any cock left in his *cock-a-doodle-doo!*"

Calliope commenced a lewd clucking and shook her sensuous tail feathers.

The Pine Bluff High School Marching Band was badly out of tune, but it was sincere. Zephyr Zendada led the band up the street to herald the start of the Helldorado Parade with a raucous, James Brown-inspired version of a John Philip Sousa march. Zephyr was wearing a lacquered straw cowboy hat with a peacock plume band, a rhinestone-studded Lone Ranger mask, and a flapping black trench coat. Every so often he stabbed the tip of his six-foot-long drum major's baton into the asphalt and twirled around it with a James Brown shout. Then, on a squealing high note from the trumpets, he whipped open the trench coat to reveal his exceedingly thin and hairy body, naked save for a pair of black fishnet stockings and a smiling jack-o'-lantern strapped across his rhythmically thrusting crotch.

Immediately following the marching band came the wigged and moose-antlered Rotarians in their shoddy Viking ship made of old refrigerator boxes and creosote-splattered beaverboard. Already drunk, they viciously hurled peppermint candy at the cowering children and beat their fists against their papier-mâché breastplates, shouting fake Swedish obscenities:

"*A saab up thy innardskivvies, ye wee teeny fartschnappers!*"

"*May Odin smurte ye, ye blusty auld codchaffers!*"

The Rotarians were followed by a squadron of equally drunk Shriners tearing around on tiny yellow go-carts. The Shriners had arrived from Fresno—a place where social prestige hinged on the consumption of vast quantities of beer, charcoal grilled meats, and ice cream. Consequently, their fifty-year-old bellies were so flabby and distended that they shuddered like jelly-filled weather balloons at every turn. Most of the Shriners were so grossly overweight that it seemed incredible the go-carts could even move them, much less zip them around at such reckless speeds. How their tassel-streaming fezzes remained affixed to their balding heads was another mystery.

Following the Shriners was a two-story-high Jack-in-the-box float sculpted from plaster of paris and old newspapers by the Mystic Order of the Ocelot, a rogue men's group that met on the second Tuesday of every month in the Vet's Hall for ritual kazoo lessons and furtive whining about their relationships with women. The head of the Jack-in-the-box bore an odd resemblance to Captain Nitt-Witt.

Right behind the Jack-in-the-box float was a covered wagon pulled by a team of sixteen freshly-shorn sheep wearing golden wings. The wings were satin—hand-sewn by the women of the Pine Bluff Pioneer's Club, who followed on a garland-strewn float emitting Bluegrass music from two speakers mounted on top of a white lattice trestle. The trestle supported a garden swing occupied by a ninety-eight-year-old woman in a navy blue ankle-length dress, Millicent Burton.

Millie, as she was known to all, had been the wife of one of Pine Bluff's founding fathers, Hephaestus Burton. This accident of marriage, combined with her longevity, had conspired to make her the unofficial Grand Dame of the Helldorado Parade for the last ten years running. Each year, the *Pine Bluff Insurrectionist* ran a feature article on her that dredged up the racy stories from her past and brought readers up-to-date on her present situation. The update was always the same. She was still mostly lucid and thought to be in good health. Occasionally she reported seeing a squid on the fencepost or claimed to have given birth to puppies, but she could still dress herself and had so far refrained from burning down her quaint little gingerbread Victorian house.

Some puffed-up old geezers in indigo blue overalls stood around on the float gawking at Millie with expressions that were meant to be interpreted by the crowd as courtly and somewhat fawning in a robust, rural manner. *Here's Pine Bluff's living history…*

More golden-winged sheep were being led on leashes by prepubescent girls in sequined ballerina costumes. One of the girls had a big silver boom box that was playing a Grace Jones tape called *Slave to the Rhythm*. The other girls did a synchronized dance to the music as the sheep looked on, chagrined.

Next came the Helldorado Queen float, and then Calliope and Mickelodia masquerading as chickens on the fat lip of Charlie the Tuna.

There was still no sign of Harley.

"That weenie," Calliope said.

28

HARLEY, HIS AGORAPHOBIC INCLINATIONS

Harley was freaking out. He wasn't getting any joy out of tree climbing anymore. In fact, he wasn't getting any joy out of anything. His Oneness with Nature had dried up on him. But that didn't mean he was ready to get down out of the trees. Every time he even thought about setting foot on the ground, he had a massive anxiety attack.

His poetry had taken a weird turn, too. He knew it wasn't a good sign to be writing the stuff he did, but he couldn't help himself. His latest effort, "Phallic Barbershop Heart Enema," had been written on the back of a yellowed postcard depicting a naked Hindu *sannyasi* projectile-vomiting purple fire and venomous snakes:

```
the smell of barbershops
made pablo neruda sob hoarsely
me too
hair tonic and aftershave
and the swimsuit issue of sports illustrated
belong to men who never doubt
their manhood
who never get sick
of their own toenails shadows and teeth
men who never feel the need for a heart enema
to flush out the umbilical cords and ashes
            *       *       *
yes robert bly
i've got a problem
but if you call me a soft male
i'll drop a tree on your fucking house
```

Harley didn't want to go anywhere near town feeling the way he did, but he had promised Calliope he would look for her in the Helldorado Parade. How she had gotten up the energy to build an entire float he couldn't even imagine. He couldn't do much more than eat and think these days without getting exhausted.

The Chicken-of-the-Sea float had traveled half the length of the parade route before Mickelodia finally spotted him.

"Look: There's Harley!" she shouted. She nudged Calliope to get her attention.

Harley was up in the enormous fig tree that shaded Cindalee's flower stand, sitting on a limb that hung way out over the street. The float was passing right under him. Calliope ran over and kicked Charlie the Tuna in the teeth, shouting, *"Driver! Stop this frickin' fish!"*

There was a squeal of worn brakes. The tuna float jerked to a halt and sat idling directly beneath Harley. He was about twenty feet above them.

Calliope smoothed her feathers and her stubby chicken wings and tilted back her chicken mask so she could address her husband:

"Harley, honey, I love you," she said, "even though you've been a total jerk to me lately."

Harley seemed fidgety. He tugged at the skin on the back of his neck and said, "Calliope, do we really have to *'cluck'* go into this right now? There's a parade going on. Besides, *'cluck'*, right now you're a chicken…."

"Harley?"

"What?"

"Shut up, sweetie…. I'm going to sing you a song." Calliope rushed over on rubber chicken feet and kicked the tuna's teeth again, shouting, *"Driver! Music, damnit!"*

From somewhere deep within the tuna's interior, a down-and-dirty blues melody began to play. Calliope reached into the corner of the tuna's mouth and emerged with an antique radio microphone on a chrome stand, which she dragged over to the place where she'd been standing before. Then, in a red hot mama voice that was like the ghost of Janis Joplin haunting a chicken suit, Calliope tilted back her head and sang the song she'd been practicing with Mickelodia all week:

> You're my studly rooster, baby,
> Yeah and I'm your willin' hen.
> Your crowin' drives me crazy,
> Honey I want you home again.
> Cuz I'm lonely and I'm blue,
> Without your cock-a-doodle-doo,
> Babe I need your cluckin' every night...

Meanwhile, Mickelodia had fished out a saxophone from the tuna's mouth. As Calliope shook off her chicken mask to stare up at Harley with her intense periwinkle eyes, Mickelodia drew on all her accumulated knowledge from two years of junior high school band classes and launched into a spastic saxophone solo.

Charlie Parker's ghost obviously wasn't taking any time out to haunt chicken costumes that day. Mickelodia bent over backward and blew a long, sustained honk that sounded like a peacock vomiting.

Harley grinned.

"Shake your tail feathers, Micko," Calliope encouraged her, glancing over her shoulder.

Encouragement was just what Mickelodia didn't need. She blew another ear-rattling honk and went into a crouch, whirling around like a Sufi dancer with an inner ear defect.

Inevitably, her rubber chicken feet tangled up beneath her. She stumbled sideways and tumbled headfirst into the tuna's mouth. The saxophone emitted a rude squawk and then went silent as the wind fled Mickelodia's lungs.

"Was that Mickelodia?" Harley asked. She'd completely disappeared.

"Yeah..." Calliope said, shaking her head. "She hasn't seen you in a while. She's a little nervous, I guess."

Mickelodia climbed out of the tuna's mouth. Her chicken mask had been left behind. Her gorgeous red hair was a mess.

"Hi, Harley..." she said meekly. Instead of waving, she flapped a chicken wing once, rapidly, like a penguin hiccupping.

"Hi, Mick," Harley said. He clucked under his breath.

"Hey! Is that Philo?" Calliope ran over to the side of the float to get a better look. "It is! Philo! Hey, over here!" Calliope jumped up and down and waved.

About one block behind them, Philo was sitting astride the neck of a gigantic blimp in the shape of a baby. It was an exact replica of what he imagined he'd looked like when he won the trophy in the Macy's Parade as an over-inflated infant.

When Philo caught sight of his mother and returned her wave, his grin could plainly be seen, even from a block away.

All those people... Harley had forgotten how crazed the Helldorado Parade could be. He hadn't been exposed to that much humanity in years. Calliope and Mickelodia, with their Horny Chicken Blues number, had made him forget about it for a moment, but as soon as they stopped the wave of humanity came crashing back on him. All that random, hectic, unceasing emotion; all the fear and hope and lust so thinly veiled by an atmosphere of cowboy-Dionysian festivity.

A guy needs a suit of emotional armor just to deal with the human species on a day-to-day basis, Harley thought to himself, clucking.

Suddenly, he panicked. There was only one limb on the fig tree that reached back into the forest. It was his only escape route. What if he had enemies? What if people were jealous of his freedom? What if a mob of angry mothers was about to come and tear down the limb, then throw turnip greens and animal crackers at him until he came down? Harley imagined himself being pelted, all the mothers of Pine Bluff jeering at him, hounding him for being a neglectful husband.

Maybe Calliope wanted to trap him.

With a scared rooster moan, Harley got up and scrambled along the limbs of the fig tree, back toward the safety of the forest.

He didn't even think to say goodbye.

Harley wasn't immediately missed. Calliope and Mickelodia's attention was on Philo. They were waving and shouting like a couple of overly-caffeinated cheerleaders. Philo waved back nonchalantly, wondering whether they sensed his newfound studliness, or if they were just glad to see him.

"Oh God! Doesn't he look great?" Calliope cried, hugging Mickelodia.

"He looks pretty cute from here," Mickelodia said, squinting. "What's he doing up on that giant baby?"

"Harley!" Calliope shouted up at the fig tree. "Doesn't Philo look more grown-up to you somehow?"

But Harley was no longer there.

"Hey!" Calliope turned to Mickelodia. "Did you see where my husband went?"

"I thought he was right here."

"That sneaky son-of-a-bitch!"

"Maybe he had to go pee," Mickelodia suggested.

"Mr. Nature Stud? He'd just whip it out and whiz right in the tree. Believe me, honey—I've seen him do it enough times."

"Well, I don't know then."

"Something weird is going on with that man. I don't like it."

Mickelodia, ever practical, said. "Maybe you guys should get some counseling."

Calliope crossed her stubby wings across her chest and stood there tapping her rubber chicken foot. "I've thought about that," she said with cool detachment. "But what am I supposed to do? Go in to see some shrink and say, 'Oh, hi, Dr. Steve!'" Suddenly she was a flirty girl of sixteen, pouting and flipping her hair. "'My name's Calliope and I'm, like, in a co-dependant relationship with a guy who thinks he's a rooster? Um, would it be okay for you to, like, climb up in a tree and talk to him with me? I know it's a huge hassle, but I'll bake you a cherry pie....'"

"No, I can see why that wouldn't work," Mickelodia said.

"Really?" The flirty girl's voice was still there. "Like, not even if I prance around in his office in a skimpy leotard and tell him I dream about dolphins?" Calliope bent over an imaginary Dr. Steve with a girlish squeal and showed him her chicken-cleavage.

At least five distinct wolf whistles were heard from the men in the crowd across the street.

29

THEOTIS, HIS BASSET HOUNDISH TENACITY

Theotis lay at his master's feet half-drunk from lapping up spilled piña coladas. There was an inordinate amount of drool oozing off the flaccid black lips of his lower jaw. He was deep in contemplation of Balmeister's right shoe. It was a tan leather wingtip with many miles on it, just ripe for chewing. Theotis really, *really* wanted to chew on something. He was longing for his rubber squeaker toy, Roberto, the Indestructible Hedgehog.

As if in answer to his longing, a psychedelic rubber hedgehog thunked down on the sidewalk just ahead of him with a breathy squeak. Theotis raised his head and looked about for other dogs. He saw none.

While not Roberto—who was a lemony yellow made dull from weeks of chewing and repeated exposures to dog slobber—the hedgehog on the sidewalk could have been Roberto's Haight-Ashbury cousin. All pink and orange and electric green, it seemed to promise new peaks of sensory stimulation, perhaps even ecstatic visions, for the dog that dared to bite it.

Theotis was that dog. He got to his feet and shook his long, floppy ears to clear his head.

Fla-whack fla-whack fla-whack went his ears—the sound of baseball cards in spinning bicycle spokes.

The act of standing up made Theotis realize he was more than half-drunk. He was totally shit-faced. The sidewalk was tilting wildly and he felt an urge to puke up his Gravy Chow all over Virginia's new Nikes. His tail went stiff. Dog spit fizzed from his jowls as if it were carbonated. A sour belch escaped him. Then the sensation of nausea passed. Theotis examined the hedgehog anew.

It was twitching.

Was it alive? Such was the state of Theotis's inebriation that he failed to notice the 30-pound-test fishing line securely fastened about the hedgehog's midriff.

Thrilled by the prospect of live prey, Theotis pounced.

There was a scuffle. The hedgehog moved with uncanny speed for a rubber squeaker toy. There was no escaping the merciless, vise-like jaws of Theotis, however. Soon the hedgehog was squeaking like an anguished chipmunk as his yellowish canine teeth penetrated its soft underbelly.

Theotis Victorious! Theotis, the Conqueror Basset Hound!

Alas, his victory was short-lived. Theotis realized the whole thing was a set-up when the surf casting rod, two stories up on the roof of Old Camozzi's Saloon, started reeling him in.

Virginia sat back with her neck resting on top of her lawn chair, arms and legs splayed in a helpless piña colada stupor. She was staring straight up at the sky.

"Sometimes the clouds look like monsters," she pronounced. "Sometimes the sky gets so blue I feel like it's going to swallow me up."

"Virginia, sometimes you talk like a woman with a paper head," Balmeister replied with a muted belch.

Theotis wasn't about to give up the hedgehog without a fight. When the fishing line jerked taut, he jerked back, growling. He leaped into the air, wriggling, as the unseen dog-fisherman tried to snap his neck. When Theotis felt slack in the line, he galloped toward a nearby newspaper rack. He wriggled under it and sat there chuffing like an out-of-shape trout hidden away in a cavern of lakeweed.

The hedgehog squeaked and spluttered as Theotis dropped it between his front paws and gnawed on it thoroughly. It was thirsty work. Fortunately, Theotis was producing copious amounts of dog spit. He paused from his labors to swallow some.

The unseen dog-fisherman was canny. A sharp flick of the line yanked the hedgehog from Theotis's paws, out toward the center of the sidewalk. Theotis gave chase. He scooped the hedgehog back up in his jaws and bore down upon it.

The surf casting rod above Camozzi's bowed sharply. Theotis found himself being hauled straight up the front of the building. He growled and clamped down even harder. He was determined not to let go of that hedgehog....

Two veterans of Pine Bluff construction crews, Thad Bickle and Ron Lowe, stood beside the wooden Indian in front Old Camozzi's Saloon admiring the asses of passing girls, rather than focusing on the parade. They both saw Theotis leave the sidewalk, his hind legs kicking the air, and then kicking all the relish off Thad's hot dog. Ron pushed back the brim of his grimy green John Deere tractor cap and watched as Theotis disappeared over the roof of the saloon.

"Damn! Did you see that dog?" Thad said, gesticulating with his molested hot dog bun.

"Sucker was flyin'," Ron flatly observed.

"I'll say."

Ron took a meditative sip of beer from his plastic Budweiser cup. "Now why would anyone be fishin' for basset hounds on a day like today, I wonder?"

Thad was philosophical, as befitted a man who had spent the last ten years of his life pounding 2x4's for yahoo contractors and asshole weekend renovators. He said, "The Kiwanis Club must've run out of hamburger patties, would be my guess."

Thad and Ron shared a ruminative chuckle over that one.

Theotis, in all his years, had never ascended the sheer face of a two-story building on a fishing line before. He found the experience exhilarating. When the surf casting rod flopped him on the flat tarred roof of the saloon, Theotis scrambled to his feet and barked, once, at the birdrobotman holding the rod. It was more an expression of feisty joy than a warning. The bark popped the hedgehog out of Theotis's mouth. It rolled behind a swamp cooler and Theotis chased after it.

Six dogs sat in a row on the other side of the swamp cooler: a mastiff, a pit bull, two dachshunds, a Yorkshire terrier, and a hairless Irish Wolfhound that Theotis recognized as Bart, Mrs. Andersen's dog. Bart and Theotis had romped and chased chickens together during Virginia's visits with Mrs. Andersen in years past. Strangely, hundreds of chickens were scattered all about the roof, walking around aloof and haughty. Bart, however, wasn't chasing them now.

The excitement was too much for Theotis. He needed a release. There were so many chickens that he couldn't decide where to begin his assault. Instead, he trotted over to the terrier and started humping her. But she was teeny and uncooperative— and with all the other dogs watching, Theotis felt foolish. He got off and skulked to the end of the line, where he stood next to Bart.

Bart wanly sniffed Theotis's butt.

The birdrobotman came down the line and strapped a little tan knapsack on each dog's back. The knapsacks had the same gunpowder smell as Balmeister's hunting vest. Balmeister had tried to teach Theotis to be a hunting dog, but that hadn't worked out so well. Theotis had an odd inclination to urinate on the birds— some instinctual idea about territorial markings gone amok....

Each knapsack had chrome antenna sticking out of it with a tiny speaker mounted near the top. When the birdrobotman spoke into a black box with red switches that he held in his fist, every dog heard his voice right behind their ears. It was not a nice voice, but it carried plenty of authority.

"Even if you have never been to obedience school, today you shall obey me," the voice said. "The Lord God commands it. It's our task to rid the world of happy hippie vermin and the small town liberals who tolerate their blasphemous ways."

All that sounded like so much gibberish to Theotis's ears, but when the voice started using words like "sit," "heel," and "attack," Theotis knew exactly what to do.

The double doors of Old Camozzi's Saloon burst wide open with a clatter of dog paws and fierce domestic barking. Theotis and Bart led the other dogs past startled parade-watchers and out into the street. The mastiff knocked over a little old lady from Pacific Palisades just two lawn chairs down from Balmeister and Virginia.

"Goddamn," Balmeister observed.

The dogs split up, each one alert and pacing back and forth with high, nervous steps, waiting for further instructions.

The speaker from Theotis's knapsack crackled to life. "Basset, attack the Viking ship," the voice commanded.

Theotis took off up the street after the Viking ship baying the long, throaty, drawn-out barks peculiar to basset hounds. It sounded like war whoops at half-speed from an adolescent Indian with a sinus infection.

"Hail! A scurvy sea monster on the starboard side!"

The Rotarians waved their cardboard swords at the charging basset hound in a boozy show of force.

"To Valhalla with ye, ye putrid-miened bandersnatch!" yelled Olaf Hernandez, owner of Olaf's Cantina, a Swedish-Mexican eatery famed for its *lutfisk* burritos.

"To Valhalla!" the others shouted in one voice.

Theotis reared up on his hind legs, paws scratching at the ship's beaverboard sides. He was barking his drunken head off.

"Out of my way, Olaf! I'll make abelskivers of the creature's innards!"

"Gizzardbitch the loathsome sneeve!"

A thicket of swords and moose antlers was thrust down at Theotis, but he just pinned back his long, floppy ears and barked even harder.

Balmeister and Virginia watched the action from their lawn chairs, not twenty yards away.

"Oh, Theotis! *Bad Dog!*" Virginia cried, waving her eighth or ninth piña colada in dismay. "Where's your manners?! Get back here!"

"What's got into that dog?" Balmeister wondered aloud. "Too lazy to chase cats, and now all of a sudden he's out there giving hell to Vikings."

"He's *your* dog. Go get him."

"Oh, Christ-on-a-corn-chip…" Balmeister groaned. The lawn chair creaked as he shifted his flabby bulk and pushed off from the arm rests.

On the roof above them, Calydon flipped a switch marked "B" on his little black box.

Down in the street, Theotis the Conqueror Basset Hound exploded.

There was a hollow boom and a huge ball of flames. The Rotarians screamed and lost their footing as the Viking ship tilted and sank on its own refrigerator box underpinnings. They waved their swords frantically as the creosote-soaked beaverboard caught fire and an oily black smoke billowed up all around them.

Balmeister resumed his seat with a sigh of relief. "Guess I won't be getting that dog after all," he muttered.

Virginia was stunned, but too drunk to be panicked, unlike most of the people around them. "Omigod…" she said in her raspy old crow's voice, "what happened?"

"You got me…."

"Basset hounds aren't supposed to just explode like that."

Calling upon his vast accumulated knowledge of dog lore and gastroenterology, Balmeister shrugged and said, "Maybe he ate a bad zucchini."

30

CALYDON, HIS HOLY TERRORIZING

O f all the atrocities Calydon had committed so righteously in his hydraulically-assisted lifetime, none had given him such pleasure as watching the Viking ship burn.

First there was the satisfying smack of the basset hound going off next to the ship like a methane-ignited piñata: fireworks of blood and flame, a slimy festoonery of basset hound entrails adorning the trees. Then the collapse and subsequent ignition of the Viking ship itself: Rotarians scurrying about like panicking jackalopes, clutching their absurd moose-antlered helmets as they jumped through fiery hoops. And finally—perhaps most gratifying of all—there was the mass hysteria engendered in the crowd: pagans on the run, heathens instilled with the fear of God, hippies freaking.

It made Calydon feel alive, full of God's juice, to be so vengeful.

Calydon spoke into his remote control box: "Wolfhound, to the marching band."

In the street below, Bart the nude Irish Wolfhound galloped past the flaming Viking ship and bore down on the Pine Bluff High School Marching Band. The band was in disarray. Tuba players danced a lumbering waltz with confounded majorettes. Piccolos peeped like lost baby birds.

Bart went into his dorky "I'm-your-buddy" routine and sidled up next to a stunned trombone player. When the hollow-eyed and melancholy young man saw Bart's tail flopping about as if it were an ecstatic, peach fuzz-covered earthworm, he instinctively reached out to pet him.

Calydon flicked a switch marked "W." Bart and the melancholy trombonist went up in flames.

A twisted trombone landed charred and smoking at the feet of a wounded Clarinet player. The remaining band members had no idea of which way to run—but they wanted to run somewhere. So when their exalted drum major, Zephyr Zendada, sprinted past them at a pace that would have put most track stars to shame, they decided to follow him.

Zephyr stayed way out in front of the other running band members, his overcoat flapping behind him like Lucifer's black wings, billowing smoke. He ran in a weird sort of ostrich jog, with his legs spraddled wide and his hands tucked down around his crotch. He was ululating as he went, wailing a long string of vaguely musical nonsense syllables, like a castrato who'd had too much to drink.

He didn't stop until he reached the front of Wilfred Lyon's General Store. There, on the sagging wooden porch, a half-dozen cowboys sat sharing a Styrofoam ice chest full of Bud longnecks. Without asking their permission, Zephyr grabbed the chest and poured the icy slush on his crotch. Steam billowed. A few Buds broke on the sidewalk.

Zephyr tilted back his head and let out a huge sigh of relief. "Thank you kindly, pardners," he crooned, wriggling his hips like an anorexic Elvis Presley. "I swear, I almost had me a hunka hunka burnin' love there."

When he set the ice chest down, the cowboys were able to see the incinerated jack-o'-lantern on Zephyr's crotch.

"You owe us three beers," drawled the tallest cowboy, "but considerin' the circumstances, we'll let it go."

And Calydon said, "The day of God's vengeance is at hand, ye lice-ridden weirdoes." Small fires dotted Pine Bluff's Main Street. The parade was in chaos. Rollercoaster waves of fear throbbed through the crowds on the sidewalks. Two dogs and a trombonist had been blown to hell and a clarinetist lay wounded. And Calydon saw that it was mean.

He was absolutely delighted.

"Pit bull, sic the Pine Bluff Pioneers," Calydon growled into his remote control box. The growling helped stifle a profound urge to snigger.

The pit bull did as he was told. He leaped onto the Pine Bluff Pioneers float, knapsack bouncing on his back, toenails scrabbling through the garlands. He trotted right over to the white lattice trestle supporting prim Millicent Burton in her garden swing. A collective frown creased the faces of the puffed-up old geezers surrounding her when the pit bull jauntily lifted a hind leg in the direction of Millie's navy blue skirt.

There was a tiny spritz of urine, then a deafening explosion as the pit pull detonated.

The blast caught Millie on the upswing. The force of it sent her flying through the air. She clenched her fists and held them tight against her sides, her body arrow-straight, teeth gritted, as she soared high above the parade route like a reluctant superhero. She was keenly embarrassed by the spectacle she was making of herself.

Look! Up in the sky! There goes Pine Bluff's living history!...

"Flap your wings, Millie, or you're a'gonna crash," hollered one of the old geezers, who had suddenly found himself sitting on his green overall-clad rump.

Millie might have flown as far as the Pine Bluff Post Office had it not been for the Mystic Order of the Ocelot's Jack-in-the-box float. But as it turned out, she plunged headfirst into the back of the Jack-in-the-box's bobbing skull and shot halfway out the left nostril of its craggy nose.

"A giraffe has spoiled my bifocals!" she was heard to say from two-stories up as she patted smooth her disheveled gray hair.

Later, when Millie was rescued, it was reported that she was still mostly lucid and thought to be in good health. She would live to tell her great-grandchildren about the experience, warning them of the dangers inherent in mysterious pit bulls and giant Jack-in-the-boxes. The great-grandchildren would listen dutifully and then ask her to tell them the story, once more, about how she gave birth to puppies.

The people of Pine Bluff had been rebellious against the Lord from the first day that Calydon knew them. Their transgressions could no longer be forgiven, for the Lord their God was a jealous God, and he could not abide a people who went whoring after Lao Tzu, yoga, herbal bath oils, Zen koans, and organic vegetables.

If it had been within Calydon's power, he would have sent a plague upon the town—a plague of frogs, lice, flies, boils, hail, locusts, and darkness; and yet another smiting plague of madness, blindness, psoriasis, hangnails, and astonishment of the heart. But such powers were incomprehensibly denied him, so Calydon had to content himself with destroying the men, the women, and the little ones of Pine Bluff with a plague of explosive dogs.

"Mastiff, take the sheep dancers," he growled into his remote control box.

The mastiff was a big, black, droopy-eared dog named Huntley who had a fondness for hard-boiled eggs and smoked oysters, which his owner fed to him on Sundays. Huntley was fortunate in that he had never been neutered, even though he had an excessive amount of dog libido. Anything was fair game: ottomans, tree stumps, neighborhood women working in their gardens.... Once the little girl next door had left her Cabbage Patch Doll out on the front lawn and Huntley had humped it beyond all recognition. He found almost everything erotic. So when Calydon gave him the command to visit the sheep dancers, Huntley found himself examining the sheep herd with somewhat reckless abandon.

One of the sheep had strayed. She had come-hither eyes and angelic golden satin wings. Huntley couldn't help himself. Before the stray sheep could utter even so much as a startled *"Baa!"* he was humping away at her wooly hind parts like a maniac.

"Uhh! Uhh! Uhh!" said Huntley in dog language. He tossed in a whispered *"I love you"* so the sheep wouldn't feel cheap.

Calydon, up on the roof, could hardly believe what he was seeing. "Mastiff! This is no time for miscegenation!" he roared into the remote control box. "God is watching from on high!"

Huntley just kept blissfully humping away. He was reaching a new sexual peak, somehow even more thrilling than his wanton hours with the Cabbage Patch Doll. No canine *Kama Sutra* manual could have possibly prepared him for this.

Calydon was furious. The remote control box was shaking in his hands. "Mastiff! This is an outrage! A perversion! You must obey!"

"Oh baby! Oh baby!" Huntley was moaning. He felt an orgasm building from the very roots of his throbbing doghood. A jerky howl of ecstasy tore loose from his throat and rose higher and higher, underscored by the lusty bleats from the sheep. Huntley shuddered as a million icy fleas bit into his flesh. This was no mere animal coupling. This was rapture, a cosmic unfolding—a Sirius supernova of bliss.

"Oh God! I'm coming!" Huntley yelped in dog language. He felt like he was about to explode.

Then Calydon flipped the switch marked "M"—and he did.

Philo had a unique perspective on the parade. From the neck of the giant baby blimp, he could see all the explosions and the resulting chaos in the street far below him *(so far his mom was okay...)*. He could also see the roofs of the stores.

Two stories up on the roof of Old Camozzi's Saloon, almost at eye-level with him, Philo saw a strange creature raving to itself and making furious gesticulations toward the street. It seemed to be part rooster, part big ugly lizard, and part knight in black and chrome shining armor. To the best of Philo's knowledge, it didn't belong there. A black and chrome lizardrooster had never been part of the Helldorado Parade before.

"Hey!" Philo shouted, to get the creature's attention. He wanted to see if he could find anything out, or at least just say hello.

Calydon cast a cold eye on the boy sitting astride the baby blimp and said into his remote control box: "Dachshunds! Take the baby blimp. Avoid all distractions." Then he slipped the remote control box behind his back and gave Philo a Heil Hitler salute.

Weird, thought Philo. *Maybe he's a cop.*

Down in the street, two tiny brown dachshunds went scampering through the throngs, practically tripping over each other in their eagerness to get under the red flatbed truck towing the cables attached to Philo's blimp. When they got there, yipping and biting at each other's tails, they both promptly exploded.

Two huge bursts of fire rocked the flatbed truck at either end and collapsed it in the middle. Philo looked down and felt himself suddenly rising into the air, way too fast. The chaos of the parade was quickly receding beneath him.

"Fuck!" was all Philo could think of to say. He was never very articulate when it came to emergencies.

31

CALLIOPE, HER WORST DIRIGIBLE FEARS CONFIRMED

"Omigod, my baby!"

When Calliope saw Philo floating away on the neck of the baby blimp high above Main Street, her whole world seemed to slow down. In the span of a few weirdly elongated seconds, she had almost a dozen semi-coherent thoughts. They went something like this:

Call the fire department.

Call the Coast Guard.

Call air traffic control.

Find an African bushman with a blowgun and get him to put a small dart in the blimp so the air will leak out slowly and Philo can land safely.

Do I know anyone who owns a helicopter?

Where the hell is Harley?

Am I a bad mother?

Why didn't I lecture Philo about the dangers of dirigibles?

I never should have tied him to the tail of that kite when he was little. That's how this whole thing got started.

I've heard of mothers lifting up whole Buicks to rescue their babies when they're in danger, but can I actually will myself to sprout wings?

No, but I can scream really loud.

"Omigod, Philo!" Calliope shouted. "Hang on, honey! We'll get you down."

☐ ☐ ☐ ☐ ☐ ☐ ☐ ☐ ☐

Philo was already too high in the sky to hear his mother's shout, but Calydon heard it loud and clear. The Chicken-of-the-Sea float was passing right in front of Old Camozzi's Saloon. While Calliope and Mickelodia stood around in their absurd chicken suits watching the baby blimp drift away (Calliope anxiously wringing her wings), Calydon zeroed in on them. "Mindless imposters," he cursed to himself. Then he spoke into his remote control box: "Terrier..." he growled, "go over and greet the nice chicken-ladies on the tuna float."

The terrier had the unoriginal name of Scotty. He had been hiding out under a fat lady's lawn chair, unwilling to participate in the action. Dogs were exploding out there. Also, the knapsack on his back reminded him of the tartan sweaters he was sometimes forced to wear for social occasions, and this thought had made him sulk in a fog of humiliation.

"Terrier, go to the chicken-ladies," the speaker on his back growled.

The fat lady shifted in her chair, trying to see what was going on beneath her massive rear end. Scotty became afraid the chair would break and he would meet his death under a quarter-ton of pink polyester. He darted out into the street.

Now he could see the chicken-ladies. They appeared friendly. Maybe they would take the sack off his back and feed him something tasty. He especially liked liver pate. And French fries. He would walk on his hind legs and bark like a circus poodle for French fries.

Scotty was out in the middle of the street when suddenly, from all directions, there was a buzzing of lawnmower engines. Scotty looked about and saw that the street was full of old men with bloated bellies and skinny legs speeding around, terrified and confused, on yellow go-carts. One was about to plow right over him.

With a yip of terror, Scotty leaped out of the way of the go-cart and almost ran headfirst into another. He dodged that one at the last instant and stopped just short of being run over by a third. Then there was a lull. Panting with dog adrenaline, Scotty ran for the Chicken-of-the-Sea float. He was almost there when he was run over by a fourth go-cart.

Scotty was already in heaven smelling French fries when his doggy body exploded.

Calliope and Mickelodia experienced the explosion as a close, frightening boom, a sudden rush of air, and a crystalline howling in their ears. They saw the front end of a go-cart erupt in flames and careen out-of-control, skidding sideways in a long, smoking arc, then shooting forward as the spindly-legged Shriner at the wheel stomped the accelerator and laughed manically. The go-cart shot over the curb in front of Old Camozzi's Saloon and smashed into the knees of the wooden Indian standing next to the doorway.

A casual observer might have gotten the idea that the Shriner had been aiming for the saloon's double doors, intent on making a dramatic entrance, and had simply miscalculated his angle of approach.

"I swear, some of those Shriners make the Hell's Angels look like wusses," Calliope said as the Shriner extracted himself from the burning go-cart wreckage and walked into the saloon scratching his blubbery white belly. His fez was on fire, but it hardly seemed to matter to him.

"Jesus, what's that?" Mickelodia said.

She was staring up at the roof of the saloon. Calydon stood there on top of the eaves, hands on his hips, black cloak billowing behind him, looking like a Romantic poet on a windy parapet—only this poet just happened to be a heavily armored roosterman. A whole flock of pissed-off-looking chickens stood on the edge of the roof with him, clucking ominously.

"Omigod," Calliope said for about the seventeenth time in the last five minutes.

"Tremble ye hippie malcontents and freethinkers!" Calydon bellowed. *"For your chicken-elders hath come to set the world aright!"*

On his cue, hundreds of chickens swarmed over the roof and went flapping down into the street. Calydon let loose with a gut-curdling rooster crow and followed them, catching air in his cloak to slow his descent.

That sucker can almost fly, Calliope thought as Calydon headed right for them. *Maybe I can talk him into helping me save Philo.*

Such thoughts went right out of Calliope's head when Calydon crashed into her and Mickelodia and started ripping the feathers out of their chicken suits.

"Gibbering barefoot wenches!" Calydon roared. "Whole-grain seductresses!" He lashed out at them with his hydraulic arms as if he meant to cripple and maim. "You lead men to ruin with your unshaven armpits and vegetarian diets!"

"What's this asshole's problem?" Mickelodia cried.

"He obviously needs to get laid," Calliope answered. She was trying to get away, but Calydon's jerks on her bulky chicken suit and her stupid rubber chicken feet were throwing her off balance. She dropped to her knees and tried to crawl.

Calydon snarled, "'It's ye who hath just laid an egg,' saith the Lord."

"Let us go, you religious creep!" Mickelodia kicked Calydon in the shin, to no avail.

"Your raiment mocks the noble chicken. For that, the Lord God commandeth: 'Make human soup!'"

"Is this guy making any sense to you at all?" Calliope, down on her knees, asked Mickelodia.

"No!" was the emphatic reply.

Calydon lurched and suddenly had them both by the scuffs of their chicken costumes. He dragged them off the tuna float and carried them, half-stumbling, up a side street toward a coal black horse buggy hitched to a team of four frothing palominos.

"Help us! Somebody! Hey!" Mickelodia shouted.

"Rape!" Calliope screamed, figuring that was the best way to get the attention of a bunch of cowboys and construction workers who'd just spent the afternoon watching dogs blow up a parade.

A few men on the sidewalk made tentative moves toward them, but no one rushed over to save the day. The big armored roosterman looked like too much of a badass for that.

Calydon ripped the backs out of the chicken suits and pulled Calliope and Mickelodia out of them like he was peeling shrimp. He handcuffed them to the railing across the horse buggy's backseat, and then he climbed up onto the driver's bench and slapped the reins. The palominos pawed and snorted and started trotting up the road toward the forest.

32

PHILO, HIS DETACHED OBSERVATIONS

Once Philo realized the baby blimp wasn't heading right into outer space—that he wasn't going to suffocate or freeze to death, and he wasn't going to fall off—an odd sort of serenity came over him. He started feeling very detached from his plight, as if his body was just on loan from some deeper part of himself that would never die. That deeper part of himself—*his soul? his spirit?*—knew he would be okay, no matter what happened. He had a kind of stoned confidence that he'd experienced only once before, when his mother went out of town to some convention for pissed-off hippie women and he'd sat around all night listening to Led Zeppelin while drinking Carlsberg Elephant Malts with tequila chasers.

The only difference was that, this time, he was pretty sure he wouldn't end up barfing his guts out all over the front porch.

It was weird to be so calm, considering the situation. He almost felt like someone else. Gone was the Philo who got scared and self-conscious and angry. Nowhere to be seen was the Philo who had a tendency to fart or wax sarcastic during magical moments.

He felt totally cool and groovy.

It was silent up there among the clouds, drifting about in an endless expanse of cool, hopeful blue. Philo was so high up he swore he could see the curvature of the earth. Far, far below him, he saw two white dots in some kind of carriage heading off into the forest. That would be the red-haired girl and his mother. He was glad they were safe. There were patches of fire and smoke all up and down Main Street.

Philo remembered past Helldorado Parades, when the frenzied afternoons wound down into warm summer evenings and everyone and their grandmother sat down in patches of tall, springy grass under the stars to watch the fireworks and discuss the meaning of life. His own grandmother, Charlene, had been present on a number of those occasions, but her metaphysics were tainted with a rabid Christianity and she always complained that the fireworks were better when she had been the Helldorado Queen, not so long ago. She spoiled it for him. Philo grew up preferring the company of other peoples' grandmothers to his own.

What was it Mrs. Andersen used to say? "The whole world may be just a teardrop in an elephant's eye, young man, and our lives pass us by in a blink. So drink your milk, say your prayers, and don't ever put dead salamanders in your mother's stir-fry again, even though we all had a chuckle about it that once."

Mrs. Andersen was like that—profound, but a realist.

A breeze picked up and pushed the baby blimp out toward the sea. The sun lay low over the blue-green horizon. Philo thought, *I am that sun. I am the sea. I am man. I am woman. I am God. I am the original rhubarb shrub. All things are within me. I already possess all knowledge. I am the still point in a turning universe. I am an intelligible sphere whose center is everywhere and whose circumference is nowhere. I want nothing. I accept everything. I am without credit cards and without fear. I am getting a little further out there than Mrs. Andersen, but that's okay—nobody's looking.*

I think therefore I am (I think of myself thinking).

I dream, therefore I am not (I dream of myself dreaming).

No, wait…. I am. I most definitely am.

I am I. I am what I am (I am Popeye the Sailor Man).

I am getting a monster headache, Philo realized, too late.

☐ ☐ ☐ ☐ ☐ ☐ ☐ ☐ ☐

Zephyr Zendada spent most of his time having thoughts like Philo's, but he never got headaches, thanks in part to the mystic healing properties of his rare Ecuadorian bonsai papaya tree buds, which scientific investigation had proven to cure glaucoma, gout, asthma, pharyngitis, and the less severe cases of ichthyosis (or fishskin disease, as it's known to the layman). The smoke of the healthful little papaya tree was also known to reduce cholesterol and high blood pressure, and to alleviate the nausea associated with chemotherapy and meals that combined beer, anchovy pizza, Mrs. Butterworth's maple syrup, and pistachio ice cream. It did, however, make you crave such things as beer, anchovy pizza, Mrs. Butterworth's, etcetera.

Zephyr was helping put out the fires from the dog explosions on Main Street. He had a big red fire extinguisher that he was enjoying immensely. Every time he pointed and squeezed the trigger, a froth of white foam spewed from the hose nozzle like testicle sauce from an ejaculating hippopotamus.

(Zephyr had recently read that hippopotamus mate underwater, that the process can take several hours, and sometimes the female has to disconnect and come up for great gulps of air. Old *National Geographics* were full of fascinating facts like that, in addition to being the best source in the world for pictures of naked African bush-ladies, to whom Zephyr had often been tempted to write soulful letters of admiration.)

Fireworks and ambulances had started to arrive on the scene. People were running and stumbling and looking for places to hide. Shop windows had been blown out, babies were crying, and all stray dogs were being eyed with suspicion, if not looked upon with outright terror. Only Zephyr remained calm. He knew there was nothing to fear. The quantity of matter in the universe never varied; all life was matter, so it followed that life could never be destroyed, only transformed into new combinations of matter in the never-ending *wu-li* dance of molecules, atoms, and quarks. Where other people saw tragedy and gruesome death, Zephyr saw one form of matter flowing into another. Fire, for instance, was just Nature's way of combining oxygen with a trombone player....

"Hey there! You! Hairy fella!"

Zephyr looked around, thinking that maybe, just maybe, the geological processes of a few million years might turn all the disposable diapers in the world's landfills into something better than diamonds.

"Yeah, you!" said a drunk old man in a wild Hawaiian shirt. "We've got us a little fire problem over here. Could you give us a squirt?"

The old man and the woman Zephyr assumed was his wife were both leaning back in orange lawn chairs clutching elaborate cocktails. On a sidewalk strewn with literally hundreds of lawn chairs, they were the only people left sitting. A large chunk of Viking ship was burning near their feet.

Pointing, the old man said, "Our damn dog did that." He was having a little tongue difficulty. He waved his free hand with airy nonchalance. "Other dogs exploded too, but ours made the biggest boom."

"Theotis was the gassiest basset I ever met," the old woman added. "We made him sleep outside."

"Not in the rain, I hope," Zephyr said, aiming the big red fire extinguisher.

"Ho!" the old man cried as fire extinguisher foam spattered his leather wingtips. He picked up his feet. After the fire had been smothered, he said, "Boy, that's really somethin'…"

"Theotis had his very own little doghouse," the old woman assured Zephyr, as if she thought he might report her to the dog police and have her arrested.

"I didn't have you figured for one of them horrendous basset hound abusers," Zephyr said.

"No, we loved our dog!" the old woman avowed.

"Shame he blowed up like that."

"It's goddamned tragic, is what it is," said the old man.

Calliope music could be heard coming from up the street.

"Say, look!" the old woman cried. "It's Captain Nitt-Witt!"

A few blocks up, near the start of the parade route, Captain Nitt-Witt appeared in Damon Squibb's old calliope cart playing a demented but somehow soothing calliope tune. The cart proceeded down the street on creaky wheels, pulled by a team of six serene zebras. As it traversed the chaos sown by Calydon—burning floats, blown-out storefronts, distraught spectators, wounded chickens—a pacifying calm seemed to descend upon everything in the cart's wake.

Zephyr's face lit up with a huge, yellow-toothed grin. The old man in the lawn chair waved drunkenly and hollered: "Hey there, Cap'n! How's it hangin'? Ate any nuns lately?"

"Bal, don't be rude," the old woman scolded.

"Sorry. I swear, I don't know who got more bombed today, me or those damn dogs," the old man muttered, while Zephyr waved his skinny arms above his head and ran in place. "Now what the hell's his problem?" He addressed Zephyr directly: "What is it? Got some bugs in your pumpkin? A case of the trots?"

Finally, the Captain spotted him. *"ZEPHYR!"* his voice boomed out—and then he laughed.

"DAD!" Zephyr yelled, blinking back happy tears. He dropped the fire extinguisher and ran up the street.

Philo had been blown so far out to sea that the shoreline had almost disappeared. When the sun went down he felt more alone than he had ever felt in his life. The blimp was drifting lower and lower, the cables almost touching the foam-flecked, darkening waves. He thought he saw shark fins below him, terrible and black, but then he realized from their rhythmic rise and fall that they were dolphins, three of them, swimming in perfect synchronization. The dolphins—and the winking, glittering lights of an airplane passing high overhead—made Philo feel less alone.

What do those dolphins think? he wondered. *Sleek torpedoes booming through a churning sea at night, their only light coming from luminous plankton, a glaring moon, the icy pinpricks of stars. Were they happy? Do they even notice me, riding a stupid baby blimp not so very high overhead?*

Would they save me if they could?

No land, no boats anywhere around him. Philo realized there was a very good chance he was going to die.

Just as he was starting to fret over what would happen to his consciousness after his body became fish food, Philo felt a weird prickling under his skin. The undersides of his arms itched. He was sprouting feathers again.

Awkwardly, Philo wrestled out of his shirt. He found that his arms alone had transformed into rudimentary wings. The feathers weren't nearly as long as they had been on the night of his owlboy flight, certainly not long enough to support him through the air, but they looked like they might do for navigational purposes. Besides, the wind had reversed.

Philo gripped the neck of the baby blimp between his legs and started flapping toward the shore.

33

MICKELODIA, HER BURNING CONCERNS

Calydon's carriage pulled into a clearing deep in the woods beyond Gargoyle Creek just as twilight was purpling the sky. A campfire crackled and licked at the bottom of a small black cauldron suspended above the flames on a tripod of metal spears. Near the clearing's edge, half-cloaked in shadows, Calliope and Mickelodia could see a gigantic wicker basket in the shape of a chicken. It sat atop of a pile of old dead tree branches as if it were nesting.

The absurdity of the whole situation annoyed Mickelodia to such a degree that she said, "Oh, give me a break...."

Her handcuffed hand was holding the railing when she spoke. Calydon turned, dropped the carriage reins, and with one swift blow, broke Mickelodia's arm. It shattered just above her wrist, hanging down grotesquely from the railing she was still gripping. There was a thick trickle of blood a few inches down from her elbow, where a triangular chip of bone jutted above her skin.

"Oh God! You sick fuck!" Calliope yelled as Mickelodia gasped and began to cry.

"Silence, you blasphemous whore!" Calydon bellowed. He struck Calliope on the jaw, knocking her unconscious.

"You're such an asshole," Mickelodia said in a quiet whimper. Then the pain in her arm hit her with its full force. A swarm of black butterflies exploded in her stomach. Her forehead turned icy cold. She leaned over the side of the carriage, thinking she might vomit, but she passed out instead.

Calydon chuckled to himself darkly and reached for the key to the handcuffs.

Mickelodia was the first to wake up. Calliope was still lying unconscious beside her. They were inside the cage of the wicker chicken's belly. In the dim light, she could make out a small door or hatch above their heads that Calydon must have dropped them through. It was padlocked. Though the loose weave of the wicker, she saw Calydon stoking the fire under the cauldron not more than a few yards away from them.

"Calliope…" Mickelodia whispered, "are you all right?"

Calliope's eyes fluttered. She groaned.

"How's your face?"

Calliope groaned again and sat up gingerly touching a dark bruise on her cheek. Then she remembered: "How's my face?" she asked, as if the question wasn't worth discussing. "How's your arm?"

"It's all swollen up, but the bleeding's almost stopped and it only really hurts when I try to move it."

Calliope examined the arm, sucking air in through her teeth. "Well, whatever you do," she said, "don't try to move it." She stood up to explore their new prison. She put her hands through the wicker and pulled, but the saplings Calydon had used in its construction were thick and green—they would give a little, but they wouldn't break. The weave was so complicated that Calliope couldn't tell where one sapling ended and the next one began. She banged on the hatch, but it was securely locked.

"What kind of sick, obsessed person would build something like this?" Mickelodia asked her.

"You got me," Calliope answered. She paused to think for a moment, and then she said, almost to herself, "Y'know, when that thing out there grabbed us, somewhere in the back of my mind I thought it all might be someone's idea of a joke. I even thought—

with the whole rooster bit—that it might be Harley in there, freaking us out a little, for a laugh, with that self-righteous Christian shit he hates so much…."

"You don't think Harley—"

"God, I hope not."

"You said he's been acting weird—even for him," Mickelodia pointed out.

"No," Calliope said resolutely; "I can't believe the man I married could be that far gone."

Calydon kept his back turned to them as he sat peeling vegetables by the campfire. There was nothing much for Calliope and Mickelodia to do but speculate upon their fate, so they speculated away. Within fifteen minutes they had concluded that Calydon intended to burn them to death. The thought did not make them happy.

"It was that crack about human soup," Calliope said; "I'm sure that's what he's planning to do to us—after we're nice and toasted."

"This is just about the best argument for vegetarianism I can think of," Mickelodia said.

"I can't believe this!" Calliope shoved and jerked against the wicker, to no avail. "I never thought I'd be burned to death. I mean, maybe if I'd been a really cool witch or something…."

"That was a patriarchal conspiracy—burning witches. It was jerk male doctors burning midwives, toady fear-mongers denying women's natural healing abilities."

"Whatever," Calliope said. She shouted over at Calydon: "Let us out of here, you big chrome turd!"

Calydon ignored her. He went right on peeling the carrot in his fist.

"It must hurt," Mickelodia speculated. "You know… burning to death."

"Just pretend you're Joan of Arc."

"Yeah, but she was tripped out on God."

"I got news for you, honey. So is our friendly RoboRooster."

Calydon approached the wicker chicken looking as if he was ready to give a sermon. He carried a flaming torch way up high in one hand and held an open Bible in the palm of the other, but what came out of his mouth certainly wasn't scripture:

"'Burn, baby, burn,' saith the Lord God of Hosts. 'Heaven hath no place for thee, ye pot smoking bimbos of abomination.'"

"I gave up smoking grass years ago," Calliope tossed back at him.

"And I never started," Mickelodia added.

"Silence!" Calydon roared. "The Lord saith, 'Shut thy traps, ye who are asinine and impudent. Ye who would turn men from solid careers as pharmacists and hedge fund managers—verily, such men as would support their infirm mothers in old age—but lo! Ye whisper in their ear: 'Let us grow organic beets, or tend to the trees of the forest.' 'Where's the money in that, for my sake?' asketh the Lord. For ye would fain forget—not only is the Lord almighty, but so, too, is the dollar!'"

"Oh, give me a break…" Mickelodia said, before remembering what had happened to her the last time she'd said that.

"I'll give thee a break, thou toilet-licking scum," Calydon snarled, thrashing the side of the wicker chicken with his torch. Sparks leaped through the weave and danced in the chicken's interior like flaming gnats.

"He hates it when you say that," Calliope told Mickelodia, just in case she'd missed the point.

"'Vengeance is Mine,' saith—"

A squeaking came across the sky.

Everyone looked up. Behind the silhouette of a 100-foot tall Monterey Pine, way up near the uppermost branches, Philo appeared sitting astride the neck of the baby blimp. He was shirtless and waving his arms back and forth in the dim light. Every time he shifted position, his legs squeaked against the blimp's rubbery surface.

The blimp drifted over the clearing, so that its underbelly was illuminated by Calydon's campfire. Philo peered down at them from behind the baby blimp's ear.

"Philo!" Calliope yelled. "This maniac's gonna burn us alive! Go get help!"

Calydon jabbed his torch into the deadwood piled under the wicker chicken. He glanced over his shoulder up at the blimp once more, laughed, and jabbed again and again. Small blazes started up in the thicket of limbs.

"Mom!" Philo shouted. With one final squeak, he half-slipped, half-leaped off the baby blimp's neck.

"Philo! No!" Calliope screamed, but too late. All she could do was watch as her son plummeted toward the tripod of spears supporting Calydon's cauldron.

34

CALYDON, HIS EMASCULATING UNMASKING

"Y ou never told me Philo could fly."

That was Mickelodia, in breathy tones of wonder. She and Calliope had watched, astonished, as Philo sprouted feathers, wings, a beak... then went flapping away above their heads like some fantastic, overgrown owl just a split-second before he was about to hit the tripod of spears around Calydon's cauldron and become the *soup du jour*, or something even worse.

"This is too weird..." Calliope breathed.

"Look at him go!"

"My son is a bird."

Philo plunged out of the sky to attack Calydon. He was a fury of feathers, all kicking feet and beating wings. Calydon cowered and bellowed under the blows.

"Get behind me, thou Satanic parakeet!"

Philo hooted and attacked again. Calydon stumbled backward and struck him a glancing blow with his torch.

"Devil-bird! Infernal grandson! Be gone!"

Unharmed by the torch, Philo gathered huge pillows of air beneath his wings and rose high above the trees. He intended to build up some serious speed before he went at the robot-rooster again. He hoped to at least knock him down on the next pass, if not kill him outright.

He could hear his mother and the redheaded girl shouting their encouragement.

"Nail him, Philo!"

"Kick His Butt!"

There was a crackling sound, like a heavy-limbed tree falling in the forest. In a sudden burst of sparks, the wicker chicken lurched and resettled itself deeper into the flames that were rapidly rising all around it. His mother and the girl screamed.

"Philo, get us out of here!" Calliope yelled. "Now!"

Calliope's "Now!" was barely out of her mouth when she heard the thump of Philo's tennis shoes landing on the wicker above her head. He tugged at the hatch with his beak and scrabbled about, but he couldn't seem to find a way in.

Calydon rushed Philo, flailing at him with the torch. Philo darted out of the way. He fluttered up into the air as the torch bashed the wicker where he'd stood just moments before.

Flames licked at the wicker chicken's wings. Choking smoke was pouring in through its breast. Calliope and Mickelodia were starting to sweat.

Calliope had bloodied her fingers on the wicker, but she still couldn't get much of an opening. Mickelodia was sitting cross-legged, holding her broken arm and muttering, "Holy fuckin' shit, we're gonna die...."

Far off in the distance, a chainsaw roared to life.

Philo soared up into the sky to peer across the top of the moonlit forest. "Dad!" he squawked, seeing Harley in the limbs of a distant tree. Harley waved his chainsaw and crowed a faint *"Cock-a-doodle-doo!"*

"Dad's coming!" Philo screeched down at Calliope. His beak made the words almost unintelligible.

Never had the familiar clinks of his father's climbing spikes and cable flip lines sounded so good to Philo's ears. As always, Harley moved with almost magical swiftness through the trees of the forest, traveling paths he'd spent years pruning and mapping out in his head. His favorite chainsaw—an orange Husqvarna 268 with a 36" bar—burbled and purred like a contented pet crocodile at his side.

When Harley reached the edge of the clearing, he hurled a golden braided tree climber's rope out ahead of him. A grappling hook was secured to the rope's end. The rope streamed out past the wicker chicken's beak and snagged in a tree beyond it. Harley pulled the rope taut and tied it off on the branch supporting him. Then he hooked a pulley from his climbing belt onto the rope and swung away.

The chainsaw roared as Harley whizzed down the rope toward the wicker chicken. Calydon was helpless to stop him. Harley swung the chainsaw in a mighty arc. Shavings exploded behind it as the saw tore through the wicker chicken's neck. Harley released the safety clip on the pulley and hit the ground rolling, the hacked-off chicken head bouncing just ahead of him. Somewhere during his flight, the Husqvarna's engine had sputtered to a halt.

"Grab the rope and climb away," Harley shouted to Calliope and Mickelodia.

Mickelodia's head was already emerging from the chicken's open throat. "Hey! Your feet are on the ground," she said.

"Harley, you're back on earth!" Calliope jeered, triumphant inside the burning chicken.

"Don't make fun of me now, 'cluck,'" Harley said.

Ignoring the pain in her broken arm, Mickelodia reached out and grabbed the rope with her good hand. She pushed off the wicker chicken's neck, using her body weight to pivot clear of the fire, then she let go of the rope and dropped into Harley's waiting arms.

"Dad! Look out!" Philo honked from the sky.

Harley turned just in time to see Calydon raising his torch to smash him over the skull. Harley ducked and ran a few strides with Mickelodia in his arms. Philo dropped out of the sky and collided with Calydon's shoulders, then flew away, knocking the big monster off-balance. The torch missed Harley's long blonde ponytail by inches.

Harley set Mickelodia on her feet and turned around, tugging on the starter cord of his chainsaw. The engine revved angrily and the chain spun. Calydon, chasing him, drew up short and drew his oversized electric carving knife from its sheath. Above them, Calliope slowly moved hand-over-hand along the rope, hoping she wouldn't be noticed before she got to the relative safety of the tree.

"'Your ass is grass,' saith the Lord," Calydon sneered at Harley.

"Whatever," Harley said, rubbing an itch on his nose with his sleeve.

They began to duel. Chainsaw clashed against carving knife. Sparks flew from gnashing metal teeth. Harley had the fluid moves of a swashbuckler from an old-time pirate movie, contrasted with Calydon's brutal, machine-like jabs and slashes.

"Long-haired wastrel!" Calydon cried, his eyes flashing black hatred and fury. "I shalt chop you up as the Cuisinart chops its foodstuffs!"

"Keep on talkin', numbnuts," Harley said, nicking Calydon's elbow with a lightning-fast flick of the chainsaw tip.

With an ear-rattling screech, Calydon slammed the carving knife down at Harley like a pickaxe. Harley blocked it with the Husqvarna's body. He whirled away and came in low, on one knee, from Calydon's left. The chainsaw revved to its full 10,000 rpms and gouged into Calydon's crotch. Blue sparks exploded off the chrome codpiece. There was a whiff of blood and burnt flesh.

Calydon lurched backward crowing horrendously. Harley eased his finger off the chainsaw's trigger and rolled away.

"Thou shalt never enter thy mother's womb again!" Calydon thundered, still standing tall as the wicker chicken collapsed into flames behind him. "My sword is God's Avenger!"

"Fuck you, pilgrim," Harley said, wiping the sweat from his eyes with the back of his work glove. He waved the chainsaw in a few modified tai chi gestures in preparation for their next clash.

Calydon attacked with savage screeches. The force behind his blows was frightening, twice what it had been before. Harley met each blow with a block or parry, but it was wearing him down. Calydon's assault was vicious and relentless. One particularly nasty blow from overhead knocked Harley to his knees. Another almost knocked him to the ground. And all the while the horrible screeches continued, bludgeoning Harley's thoughts the same way Calydon intended to bludgeon his head.

Unnoticed by either of them, Calliope had climbed down out of the tree that Harley's rope was hooked into, and now she was running over to the campfire where Calydon's cauldron still hung from the tripod of spears. She grabbed a spear and shook it loose from the others. The cauldron went tumbling. Paying no attention to her scalded toes, she let loose a fierce cry of pagan womanhood and charged Calydon from behind.

Calydon turned and saw her coming. He could have skewered her with one sure thrust of his carving knife if Philo hadn't dropped on him from out of the night.

Wings beat in Calydon's face. Feathers obscured his vision. *"Ghah! Cursed owlboy!"* he roared, swinging his arms wildly.

Philo cried out. Calydon's carving knife caught in his left wing and dug into it with the sickening sound of a meat saw hitting bone. He wrenched himself free and went half-flapping, almost crawling his way through the air, until he disappeared into the dark forest at the clearing's edge. There was a crashing of tree branches and a thud that seemed to come up out of the ground—and then nothing.

In the stillness of that moment, Calliope harnessed every bit of her anger at the monster that had threatened her husband and hurt her son. "You asshole!" she screamed. She hoisted her spear like some berserk Zulu warrior-woman and drove it right through Calydon's armor, deep into his breast.

Calydon bellowed and went down on his side, clutching at the spear that was lodged so close to his heart. Calliope put both hands on the spear's end and rammed it in even deeper.

"Finish that bastard off," Mickelodia said, coming up beside her. "I'll go make sure Philo's all right."

Harley kicked the carving knife out of the way and shut off his chainsaw. "Man. Way to go, Clippy..." he said with a low whistle.

"Didn't I tell you I hate that name?" Calliope said, grinding the spear in with the full weight of her body. Calydon twitched and shuddered beneath her like a pinned bug.

"Sorry. I didn't mean to condescend. Whew!" Harley stooped by Calydon's head. "Let's see who you shish-kabobbed here."

He unscrewed a few wingnuts and tugged on Calydon's mask.

There was a moment of stunned recognition.

"MOM!" Harley exclaimed.

The gasping, sweaty face of his own mother was right there—wild-eyed with pain and steroid abuse—inside Calydon's armor.

"Charlene!" said Calliope. "Goddamn you!"

"So what? *SO WHAT?!*" Charlene said, her voice tiny but still mean without her amplifier.

Harley had a look of concern on his face that made Calliope want to slap him. "Mom," he said in his sincerest tone, "how long have you been this evil über-rooster? *'cluck'*"

Charlene rolled her eyes and sighed, as if she knew she was dying and considered explanations trivial.

"I had the suit made for me by an alcoholic welder in Palmdale. But I've always been a rooster. When I was a little girl, I'd eat worms for a nickel."

"So it's *'cluck'* hereditary?"

Calliope draped her arm across Harley's shoulders and said: "That's right, honey…. You may've fried your brains on drugs, but you're a rooster because your mom's a flipped-out, God-fearing, Jesus-freakin' psycho-puppy!" Then she got right in Charlene's face. "You are the mother-in-law from hell, do you know that? I'm sorry I ever invited you over for Christmas."

"Your non-dairy eggnog was atrocious," Charlene spat back.

"Better than that cardboard piece of crap you called a fruitcake!" Calliope grabbed the spear in Charlene's chest and wiggled it. Charlene howled in pain.

Harley grabbed Calliope from behind. Calliope flailed against him with her knees and elbows—close to hysterics now that the danger was past. Then she relaxed and allowed Harley to hold her.

"Mom," Harley said over Calliope's shoulder, "can you tell us why you were on such a rampage? I mean, *'cluck'*, you blew up half of Main Street. And all those dogs. And that poor trombonist."

"I bragged to all my friends that you were going to be a pharmacist in a quaint New England town—"

"—where they still swept the sidewalks," Harley filled in for her.

"You were going to take care of us both…."

Harley sighed. He still had some unresolved co-dependency issues with his mother, obviously. But it seemed a little late for therapy.

Charlene grew indignant. She pointed a hydraulic finger at Calliope and snarled: "But then you met this little flower power tramp."

"After that, it was 'Death To All Hippies,' huh?" Calliope looked to Charlene for confirmation. Then she turned to Harley and said: "See? I told you she never liked me."

Incredibly, a merry-go-round song started up from somewhere deep in the forest. It sounded like a band of leprechauns playing panpipes, flutes, and bassoons. Or maybe an ice cream truck was headed their way.

"I hate this town," Charlene grumbled. "I hate everyone in it. If I had my way, I'd put it all in a box and bury it."

"She'll be going into her 'Scum-of-the-Earth' routine pretty quick here…" Calliope murmured into Harley's ear.

"I could have done it too. I could have buried you all, but—"

"Cluck?" Harley queried.

"—the commute was killing me."

Charlene's head lolled to one side and her life leaked out of her like the sour, dusty air from a punctured inner tube. She still looked mean, even in death.

Captain Nitt-Witt and Zephyr rolled into the clearing on the zebra-drawn calliope cart. The Captain raised his hands off the keyboard and waved to Harley and Calliope.

"Hey there! Sorry about your mother, Harley," he said with gruff good cheer. "Can't say I ever liked her, though."

"That's okay," Harley said. "She was kind of a bitch."

"Anybody seen Philo?"

"Omigod, Philo!"

Calliope had been saying that a lot lately.

35

CAPTAIN NITT-WITT, HIS BUTTERFLY DREAMING

Calliope's first thought was that Mickelodia was giving Philo mouth-to-mouth resuscitation. He was on his back with his head in Mickelodia's lap, his face lost in the canopy of her silky red hair. However, Philo seemed a little too active to be in need of that kind of emergency attention. In fact, as Calliope observed her son's right hand sneaking up to cup Mickelodia's breast, it occurred to her that Philo was acting downright frisky.

"Philo!" Calliope shouted.

Philo and Mickelodia paused briefly to acknowledge her, but they weren't about to stop kissing.

Philo's mid-air collision with a carving knife and subsequent crash-landing had left him with a broken arm and various cuts and abrasions, but overall, none of it seemed very serious. Certainly there was nothing so very wrong with him that he was going to let it get in the way of his re-acquaintanceship with Mickelodia. She was the most magical being he'd ever set eyes on. He felt like everything he'd been through in his life had been just a prelude to their reunion.

Mickelodia shared Philo's sense of destiny. He was the winged prince from her dreams, her twin in love. As if their bodies were reflecting this knowledge, Philo's arm had been broken in exactly the same place as her own.

Later, after their bones were mended, they would share similar scars.

☐ ☐ ☐ ☐ ☐ ☐ ☐ ☐

A loving family is the best, most precious thing a person can have. If Harley had learned nothing else, at least he had learned that. Never had he been more grateful for having a wife than when Calliope put a spear through his mother. And when he thought about what Philo had done, dive-bombing out of the sky to save everyone, Harley could only marvel at what heart his son had. And what guts! Not to mention those crazy wings....

From that moment onward, Harley knew where his loyalties had to be. He moved back home with Calliope and Philo, never to spend another night in the forest alone.

He gave up tree trimming to become a wood sculptor, spending most of his mornings up at Nitt-Witt Ridge, where Captain Nitt-Witt taught him the intricacies of carving. Harley's technique would never get to be quite so refined as the Captain's (he'd never figure out how to get his own carvings to just drop out of the ceiling, for one thing...). But as time passed and Harley grew more confident in his own artistry, he liked to think he made up for his lack of refinement with sheer scale.

Starting with the trunks of massive fallen trees, Harley roughed out a shape with his chainsaws, then proceeded with more traditional carving tools to sculpt a host of fantastic creatures: hippogriffs, sirens, trolls, Chinese dragons, basilisks, squonks, and so forth. His goal was to make at least one statue of everything Jorge Luis Borges had described *The Book of Imaginary Beings*.

Soon these statues were selling at the Pine Bluff Trading Post, and Harley had an income that surpassed what he used to make as a tree trimmer. He and Calliope saved up enough money to travel the world. They disguised themselves as gypsies, so they could go anywhere they wanted without getting hassled. Harley was able to visit all of the places where his favorite authors had grown up. Calliope found a lot of great new gardening ideas.

Harley also gave up his postcard poetry after he stopped living in the trees. He started listening to reggae music instead. He found he just wasn't lonesome enough to dredge up those weighty words from the dark well of his soul anymore. He no longer needed the words, content as he was now with life itself.

Philo and Mickelodia eventually decided to get married—a decision that surprised no one. But they knew they were young, and they weren't in any hurry. First Mickelodia enrolled in the University of California at Santa Cruz to study Jungian psychology. Philo joined her there a year later. They both ended up with graduate degrees from the History of Consciousness program. Engaged without mishap the entire time, they finally moved back to Pine Bluff to take their vows.

The wedding took place on Gargoyle Creek. Not beside or near the creek, but actually on the creek, with Philo and Mickelodia standing barefoot in water up past their ankles, and the Reverend Zephyr Zendada right beside them, wearing a kilt.

It was a beautiful ceremony. Mickelodia wore an angelic white gown with an almost endless train that floated way out behind her on the water. Philo looked charming and dangerous in his English tuxedo. White candles burned in the boughs of trees, on floating lily pads, and on every available rock. Calliope had strewn bright bouquets of wildflowers everywhere.

Almost everyone in town gathered in the forest to watch the ceremony and wish the new couple well. Even the sun seemed determined to be a part of the proceedings. Somehow it broke through the tangled bower and dappled its light on everything.

Harley had the honor of giving away the bride. Philo's Aunt Virginia and Uncle Balmeister played Hayden's "Wedding March" on a funky upright piano and made it sound fabulous. They were both already sloshed, but their happiness was real and infectious. Harley gave Mickelodia a kiss on the cheek as he handed her over to his son along with a stealthy thumbs-up signal.

Zephyr cleared his throat and addressed the crowd in a voice loud enough for everyone to hear:

"During the course of my long and hairy travels, I met me a Hindoo fella by the name of Parmesan Yoga-somethin' who said God'd told him: 'By bein' happy, my child, thou doth please me.'" Zephyr paused to let that sink in, then he stated the obvious:

"These two young folks here are just about the happiest people I ever seen."

A murmur of agreement passed through the crowd.

Zephyr looked straight at Philo and Mickelodia and flashed them a gopher-toothed grin. "You both wanna get married?"

Philo and Mickelodia looked deep into each other's eyes.

"I do," they said simultaneously.

Calliope let out a sob that sounded like a walrus belching.

"Well now!" Zephyr declared. "As an Immaculately Ordained Sex-Priest of the Church of Free Love and Fine Thinking, I do hereby declare you both married in the eyes of God and everybody here. Philo, you may kiss yer bride."

It turned out to be one heck of a kiss.

"Way to go Philo!" Harley said, raising his fist in salute. If he'd had a chainsaw along with him, he would have fired it up and waved it.

Later, after a solid hour of hugs and kisses and manly handshakes in a seemingly endless greeting line, Philo's Aunt Virginia and Uncle Balmeister came up to Philo and Mickelodia and handed them two first-class airline tickets to the French Riviera for their honeymoon. A chateau in Nice was reserved in their name for a full two months, Balmeister explained. When Philo and Mickelodia tried to thank him, he said it was nothing, just a small perk of the international real estate game.

It was the Captain, however, who had the biggest surprise of the day. During a round of toasts at the reception, he announced that he was giving Philo and Mickelodia the deed to Nitt-Witt Ridge.

After the applause subsided, Philo took the Captain aside for a private conversation:

"You can't do this, it's your home," he said.

"Are you gonna kick me out on the streets like some vicious slumlord?" Captain Nitt-Witt asked him.

"No. But what about Zephyr? He's your son."

"Zeph and I already talked it over."

Zephyr leaned in over their shoulders and cheerfully said, "I just wanna keep travelin' down that old Road to Nowhere. All's I need is a promise you'll keep a bedroom open for me when I'm passin' through."

"Of course." Philo didn't know what else to say.

"Look, Philo," the Captain said, hugging him, "I'm an old, old man. I need to catch up on my dreams a little, and then I'll be heading out to the marble orchard. I'm doing this because I know you'll take care of the place. Keep up the memories. And eventually, I want you to make it your own."

Philo thanked him and said he'd do his best.

The Captain assured him that would be more than good enough.

True to his word, Captain Nitt-Witt began spending more and more time asleep. Sometimes he didn't get out of bed until late afternoon. It seemed perfectly natural. After all, bed was where he discovered himself when he woke up, he felt fine there, and he could think of no real reason to leave.

When he wasn't dreaming, the Captain usually reached over to his bedside bookcase and grabbed something to read—either the writings of Chuang-Tzu or, more often, a full-color encyclopedia of butterflies. He liked to lay there with the warm afternoon sunlight slanting across his lap and lose himself in pictures of Swallowtails, Hairstreaks, and Spread-winged Skippers. Sometimes he would stay in bed turning pages until it got dark and he could go back to sleep.

Harley checked in on the Captain every day while Philo and Mickelodia were away one their honeymoon. Strange things were happening in that bedroom. The Queen's Luce ivy growing out by the window had found its way inside. Dark, waxy green leaves were sprouting on the walls, crawling their way across the ceiling. It was like a greenhouse in there, hot and muggy.

When Philo and Mickelodia returned, the door to the Captain's bedroom would barely open. Philo had to go in through the window to give him the news that Mickelodia was carrying a new addition to the Marndog family. Captain Nitt-Witt burrowed deeper into his cocoon of blankets with a smile and a sigh as he offered Philo his congratulations.

Then he fell fast asleep.

Philo tiptoed across the room to the door. The carpet was spongy with toadstools and clover. On the nightstand, a mossy antique radio was tuned to a station quietly playing jazz from the thirties. Somewhere a frog croaked, perhaps from inside one of the Captain's old brogans. A snail caressed a shoehorn. Two slugs made love on top of a red woolen sock. Under the bed, exotic lilies and orchids bloomed, their petals huge and luminous, like the life in them had turned to light.

As Philo tugged on the doorknob, Captain Nitt-Witt began to snore.